# 31 Spells for October

A month of horror stories to conjure.

BRIAN JAMES LANE

31 SPELLS
FOR OCTOBER

*For Brandon, my artistic pal.*

*Thank you for being a friend.*

# Table of Contents

*"Those who don't believe in magic will never find it."*

*– Roald Dahl*

# STAY AND SIT A SPELL

## *October First*

"Don't take to the moon, much. I don't care if it is full. Prefer my feet grounded and head out of the clouds, thank you very much," said Adélaïde Rieux.

The old witch glared at the werewolf. His fur was matted with drying mud and scum from the swamp outside. He glared but couldn't growl. He couldn't do much of anything after her spell.

The werewolf was paralyzed and rigid, yet completely aware of his surroundings. His arched form was comical – suspended in midair and frozen in the moment of his attack. Adélaïde laughed at him.

"Look at you. Scary ole beasty come down to eat up an old lady. Some old ladies won't take to that, either. Me being one that can do something about it," she scolded.

The eyes of the werewolf followed her. The pure animal hatred had left. There was a touch of humanity in them now. And fear.

Adélaïde said, "Maybe I should eat you. How'd you like that?"

The werewolf whined. It tugged at her heartstrings. "Ahh, you silly thing. I don't have the heart to eat such a lovely creature. But I sure put a whammy on you, I'm afraid. Take a month to wear off."

The werewolf whined again. Adélaïde sighed. The monster had startled her and sometimes she just didn't know her own strength.

"I'm sorry. I don't have a counter spell. Just have to wear off. But, the good news is that I'll finally have me some company whilst I cast a few spells."

The old witch walked up to the werewolf, gently stroking his dark fur. She took a withered old tea towel and dipped it in her boiling cauldron, currently only heating water for her laundry. Adélaïde lovingly wiped muck from the werewolf's thick coat.

"I tell you what I'm going to do, wolf. So you don't get bored, I am going to tell you a story about each of the spells I am going to cast. One a day until Halloween. How'd you like that?" she asked.

Though the werewolf couldn't reply, she could swear she saw a twinkle in his eye. Adélaïde grabbed her spellbook and opened to the first page.

# SOMETHING FAMILIAR

*Still October First*

"It's true. The cat was on the fence when Bess passed. I saw it again outside of Carolina's window just before she died," Maude said.

Ruth tried to calm her old friend. "This is an assisted living home, Maude. People die here all the time. I am sure the cat was just a coincidence."

"I'm telling you, Ruth. The creature is a harbinger. Some kind of familiar. It brings death," Maude explained.

"Okay, Maude. I am not going to argue about the existence of evil portends. I will warn you that if Nurse Chelsey hears your diatribe, she may up your medication or worse – isolate you. You don't want that, do you?" Ruth said.

Maude's eyes grew worried. Ruth patted her hand reassuringly. "I'm sorry, dear. I am not trying to scare you. I just want to remind you. We have little control over our surroundings. Our reactions are a small measure of control, so we have to keep our wits," Ruth said.

"I have some control, Ruth. That is what I've been trying to tell you. I've done something to protect us," Maude whispered.

This concerned Ruth. What could she have done? "What?" she asked.

"I've set a trap. I made a snare out of some copper wire and set it on the fence outside our window. If that harbinger tries to lure death to us, it is going to be in for a big surprise."

"What? Show me," Ruth said, grabbing Maude by the arm.

After some cajoling, both of the women left the common area and headed back to their room. To their surprise, the snare had already done its job. Hissing at them from behind the glass was a black cat. It saw them and panicked. It scrambled to free itself, which resulted in garroting off its own paw. The bloody limb remained in the trap.

"Oh, how awful," Ruth said and feared for the sanity of her roommate.

The next day, Nurse Chelsey changed that perception. When she came to check on them, her left arm was wrapped at the wrist where she was missing a hand. When she glared at them, the pupils of her eyes were narrow slits.

# BOGWATER

## *October Second*

The old witch was waiting. She knew he would be coming soon. Tendrils of smoke wafted up from the fire in the middle of the room. The ghostly shoots struggled to escape through the hole in the middle of the thatch roof, long since overgrown with moss and lichen. Once outside, the smoke would point the way to her hut. She knew he would be coming soon. The old witch waited patiently.

Fred Johnson slapped absently at another bloodsucking mosquito. He hated the fowl creatures. Why must he visit the witch in the middle of night, anyway? He honestly wondered how much was for show and even if there was any credence to her abilities at all. He felt as if he had nothing left to lose, though. The risk was worth it.

The full moon shone brightly, though not always illuminating the path. The lush canopy of Cyprus trees shielded all but the most stubborn of moonlight from reaching the modest trail. At times, Fred had to step on the bulbous roots of the trees to keep from getting his feet wet in the marshy undergrowth that sprung from the trail. He must be getting closer to the swamp.

Fred pushed the low hanging strands of moss and leaves out of his way, weary of any nocturnal snakes which may be hanging from the lower tree branches. He was about to give up when he saw wisps of smoke glowing from the moon like mournful spirits. He had found the shack.

Crossing from the trail into the swamp proved more treacherous. Fred saw that the old witch had a small dock and rowboat off to the side, but it did not moor with the shack itself, so it was of no use to him. He had to gain access to the hut by trudging through the sludge.

Splashing loudly through the bog, Fred heard the cacophony of frogs, crickets, and other unknown creatures of the swamp. It certainly had an atmosphere conducive to a belief in the occult. The old witch probably would not have been so successful at her charge had she lived in an urban setting.

Fred was close enough to see the yellow glow of firelight through the planks in the wood of the shack. There was a small porch attached to the one room house. An old tree trunk served as a chair outside.

There were gourds, dried flowers and plants hanging from a cross beam.

He pulled himself onto the porch, using one of the log pillars that supported the roof. A large rat scurried off, splashing into the swamp. Fred left muddy wet footprints on the wooden floor of the porch as he walked up to the front door. He took a deep breath and reached for the piece of rope that served as the handle. He didn't bother to knock. She would be expecting him.

As if to verify this, the old witch beckoned from within, "Come in."

Her voice was raspy and thick as if the humid air clung to her vocal chords as it had everything else in the swamp. Fred pulled the rope, which raised the wood slat from within. He crossed the threshold into the witch's abode.

She sat near the glow of the fire in an old rocking chair. She poked and prodded at the flames with a long stick, which sent sparks dancing upwards to the small hole in the ceiling. Either she enjoyed the primitive atmosphere or the witching business was not as lucrative as one might imagine.

"Sit," she said, indicating another tree stump next to her.

The old woman's black skin hung loose and leathery over most of her frail form. It was wrinkled and slightly reptilian in appearance, especially around her neck. Her hair was a messy nest of unkempt white Afro, which shot wildly from her small head. Her eyes were milky white with cataracts. Her hands were skeletal in appearance where the skin was stretched tight across knuckles swollen with arthritis.

"Sit," she commanded again.

Fred walked hesitantly to the spot beside the old woman. Her small body was in direct contradiction to the presence she personified. This woman had power, and it was obvious. He sat down on the stump, grateful that he could use the fire as an excuse to gaze into rather than into the milky depths of her eyes.

The old woman ineffectually cleared the phlegm from her throat. "Payment first."

Fred fumbled through his pockets, withdrawing several crumpled bills. He extended them in a wad towards the woman. Her arms did not reach for the money. Instead, she nodded towards a table next to her. On it, a wooden bowl held several coins and bills. There were even some gold fillings as payment, he noticed. Fred dropped the money into the bowl and sat back down.

He could already feel the warmth of the fire drying his wet pant legs in the front. It made his legs itch slightly.

"Good," she said.

"I understand you can get rid of people. Make them disappear," Fred stated.

The old woman nodded. "Yes. That is my specialty."

"His name is MacIntyre. Brian MacIntyre. My parole officer."

The old woman grunted, nodding in understanding.

"He's the one I want to disappear. He's been making my life miserable ever since I got out of prison."

"I understand, child. But won't they just assign you a new parole officer when Brian MacIntyre disappears?"

Fred nodded, "Yeah, I suppose so. Doesn't matter much, though. Can't get much worse than MacIntyre. He takes this personally. He thinks I should not have been granted parole – that nobody should. He has a vendetta against me. I am honestly trying to turn it around this time. He doesn't believe me. He won't give me a chance, sticking around and making it difficult for me to get a job and-"

"Okay, okay. Yes. I see. Let's start, then."

The witch got up and shuffled through a chest in the corner of the room near a pile of straw that must have served as a mattress. She eventually returned, holding a small tin coffee mug. In her other hand, she grasped other items that Fred couldn't immediately identify.

Fred's pant legs were almost completely dry in front. He tried to shift so that the back of the pant legs would dry out as well. She glared her opaque, filmy eyes at him. Her wide nose crinkled.

"Give me your hand," she demanded.

The old witch produced a dagger from a hidden pocket in her billowy cloak. "Look, lady. I know you're powerful. I respect that. However, I'm not just going to let you stab-"

Cackling laughter interrupted Fred. He shut up. She shook her head with the laughter.

"Boy, I'm not going to stab anyone. Do you want this Brian MacIntyre gone?"

Fred nodded. "Good. Then give me your hand," she insisted.

Fred remained motionless. The old witch scoffed.

"Look," she said, "I have a nephew who is a good boy but has had a run of bad luck, too. With a record, he can't seem to make any headway. I understand, child. I understand."

With that, the old witch gently pulled his hand towards hers. Her grasp was firm, yet somewhat reassuring. His mistrust of the woman abated; he nodded.

The old witch ran the blade across his palm, unleashing a torrent of blood. She greedily caught the flow with the metal cup. Fred withdrew his hand, pulling it from her bony grasp. He pulled his shirt untucked and used a bottom corner to stop the bleeding.

The old woman smiled, revealing a few ragged teeth amongst her putrid gums. She held the cup near the flames of the fire. With her other hand, she began to sprinkle ingredients into the cup.

"To the blood, root of Mandrake and powdered bone. Scales of snake and small pine cone. Potion gets hot, must get hotter so that I can boil it all in – damn it."

Fred looked at the witch, confused. She cursed again. "Damn it!"

"What? What is it?" he asked.

"Potion gets hot, must get hotter so I can boil it all in bogwater."

She sat back, pulling the cup from the flames. "Bogwater. I need bogwater."

Fred nodded feverishly. "Yeah?"

"I don't have bogwater," she said.

Fred Scowled, "You live in a swamp!"

The old witch nodded in agreement. She thrust the cup to Fred. "Get me some bogwater."

"What?"

"Go out near the boat and scoop up some water from the bog," she instructed.

Fred scoffed, sighing deeply. Grudgingly, he accepted the cup and retreated from the confines of the shack. The chorus of swamp creatures bid him welcome back into the humid night.

Fred's pant legs had just dried out, of course. Now, he had to jump back into the shallow waters. What difference did it make if he got the water from here or from the boat? He reached down with the cup.

"Near the boat," she reminded him again, shouting in her hoarse voice.

Silly witch, he thought. Fred traipsed to the side of the house. He sloshed through the water.

Lily blooms shone bright blue in the moonlight. They gently drifted away out of his path as he crossed, leaving a pleasant aroma that momentarily masked the putrid swamp odor.

The dock was partially submerged. The soft muddy ground must have not been a strong enough foundation for the wooden structure. Fred stepped on it, feeling its uneven surface. He hoped that the dock was strong enough to support his weight. It gave slightly, but had a semblance of support.

Fred neared the end of the dock adjacent to the boat. This must be far enough to suit her needs, he decided. Fred bent down to scoop up bogwater from the swamp. The cup dipped into the water.

Instantly, the dock he stood upon came alive. An enormous head swung around from under the watery depths. It's large jaws opened, revealing jagged fangs. Its tail spun around. The speed and ferociousness of the attack, coupled with the mere scale of the creature, had stunned his unbelieving mind. Fred fell from the moving surface into the swamp. The monster attacked.

It rolled with its prey, tearing flesh and splintering bones as it attempted to drown the victim in the swampy bog. Fred never had a chance to scream, much less flee. It was over in a few short bloody moments.

The old witch smiled. She heard the creature doing its job outside. The loud thrashing about made her cackle. The arrangement was simple. MacIntyre was happy to be rid of the "scum", as he called them. The old witch continued to keep Todd, her nephew, out of jail. And Bogwater, her beloved pet, got a steady diet of fresh meat.

The thrashing ceased and the mammoth alligator emitted a satisfied roar. The old witch nodded in agreement. Now, she just had to wait. She knew another would be coming soon.

## STILL LIFE AND DEATH

### *October Third*

Harvey bought the painting at the street fair. The artist had done it in 15 minutes. Although not anything that could be classified as fine art, the price was right.

Then, he heard the rumors. The artist, a man by the name of Fredric Morrow, had been famous once. Now infamous, he was reduced to selling his art for pennies on the dollar at third-rate markets.

Had Harvey known, he would have steered clear of the old coot. Legend had it that the paintings commissioned for Fredric Morrow had a dire consequence. The curse affected the subjects of the oil on canvas paintings.

Fredric had painted the crown jewels for some Eastern European Monarchy. An inept burglar wound up blowing the jewels away along with the safe in a botched burglary. Another story said that Fredric painted a landscape of the Yurmich Bridge in Washington State. That bridge collapsed, killing four people in the process. There were more tales but to less notable yet nonetheless calamitous outcomes.

Fredric only painted still life studies and landscapes. But, his hunger must have outweighed his preference that fateful day at the street fair. Harvey had requested that his portrait be painted. Fredric had complied. The painting was currently adorning the space above the mantle on the cavernous fireplace in Harvey's estate.

Harvey stared at himself, who stared back through canvas chasms as deep as time and space. The pigment was somehow mesmerizing him. Harvey (the one made of flesh and bone) shook his head to clear the effect.

"No," he proclaimed.

He approached the painting, intending to burn it. He stepped on the hearth and leaned over the mantle standing on tiptoes to reach the bottom edge of the portrait.

That is when his clothes dipped into the fireplace. The screaming lasted only a few minutes. It was enough to warn the servants and have the fire department salvage most of the mansion. Harvey, however, was completely immolated.

Fredric Morrow, no doubt going by a nom de plume, still paints at street fairs across the country. He has added portraits of pets and people to his repertoire. His prices are reasonable, but don't take him up on them.

## THE CLAWFOOT BATHTUB

### *October Fourth*

Ouida Shrader found the piece in an antiques shop while on vacation. It was during a driving trip over the summer. It had taken weeks to ship, but finally it was here. And none too soon. The first snowfall of the year had just come. What better way to spend it than soaking in an antique clawfoot bathtub?

Spending Saturday night in a bathtub might seem boring for some. Not for Ouida, though. Her favorite pastime was relaxing and curling up with a book.

Her husband Paul was working this weekend. Ouida would be all alone. It was how she preferred it.

The workmen finished installing the tub in the upstairs bath. They hauled away the old tub. Ouida tried to tip the hard-working men, but they would have none of it. They said her husband had taken care of everything.

The place was all hers.

Ouida filled the basin with hot water and suds. Though it was still before six, she poured herself a glass of merlot. She found a paperback and slipped into the bath.

She sighed, closing her eyes. Instantly, she had visions of being drowned in the tub. Through a dream-like state, she could barely see the blurry outline of someone holding her underwater.

Ouida opened her eyes. What had the vision meant? Had someone been murdered in that bathtub?

She got out and dried off. Ouida could not shake the feeling that she had witnessed some past horrific event. She had to learn the history of the clawfoot tub.

The antique shop had no further information other than the approximate age of the bath. Ouida was frustrated. Normally, when she was stressed, she would soak.

The next day was Sunday. Paul would return tomorrow. She decided to try one more time.

Ouida got into the hot, foamy tub. Nothing happened. She closed her eyes.

The vision returned. Someone was drowning her. She opened them.

Paul was there, standing over her. He frowned. Ouida opened her mouth to say something.

He grabbed her, pushing her under. It was the same vision coming true. Ouida realized the bathtub did not show her something that happened but something that was going to happen.

# AUNT DORIS AND THE HALL CLOSET

## *October Fifth*

J.J.'s mom, Selma, was making a caramel macchiato or something for a customer when she saw them walk in. Officer Steve James, a boy from the neighborhood, had trouble when he was younger but grew up to serve and protect. J.J. liked Steve, but under the circumstances he wished he weren't there. J.J. was still in the "having trouble as a boy" stage of his life.

Normally, Selma would be pleased to see him. Sometimes, she might even sneak him a free hot chocolate. But not today. Today, Steve was there to talk to J.J.'s mother. Selma was going to be steamed.

Selma waved at Steve and tried to smile. It came across as a pained smirk. She finished making the drink and took the money. With no other customers in line, she took off her apron and announced she was taking a quick break.

She came up, whispering to them. "What have you done now, J.J.?"

J.J. responded, "Mom, it wasn't me."

Officer James interjected, saying, "Mrs. Johnston. Sorry to bother you at work."

"It's okay, Steve. What happened?" Selma said.

"Umm, Officer James, please. I'm on duty." He said.

J.J. looked at Steve. He looked uncomfortable and embarrassed. J.J. felt sorry for him, but not as sorry as he felt for himself.

"Yes, sir. Sorry. What has my son done this time, Officer James?" Selma said.

"He was caught shoplifting at the video game store down the street. There were some older kids with him, but they ran off." Steve said.

Selma closed her eyes and took a deep breath. J.J. knew he was in trouble. She couldn't even find the words to speak.

Steve continued, "I managed to talk the owner out of pressing charges."

Selma replied, "Oh, thank you so much Ste - Officer James."

"You're welcome, ma'am. However, this is the third time. Next time, I will have to write a report. I can't keep covering for him," he said.

Selma nodded. She smirked. "I understand. You're doing your job and you need to be consistent. J.J.'s just not taking his father's death so well. That's an understatement. Neither am I. I wish I could take some time off, but we just can't afford it. Aaron didn't have insurance. His pension just barely covered the funeral and-"

J.J. watched as his mother came apart, sobbing. Steve put an arm around her. He looked at J.J., motioning for him to do the same. J.J. hugged his mom, sheepishly.

Steve said, "We all miss your husband, Mrs. Johnston. He was a good man...and so is J.J. He's really a good boy, Mrs. Johnston. He's just fallen in with the wrong crowd. That's all."

Selma wiped away tears from her cheeks. She even managed a smile for J.J. Maybe he wasn't in so much Dutch after all.

"I know he's a good boy. Takes after his father, all right. I wish he could stay at home, but there ain't much for him to do there," Selma said.

"Is there anywhere he can go? Anyone to look after him?" Steve asked.

J.J. could tell his mom was thinking of something. He couldn't figure out what it was, though. She said, "Maybe. We had a falling out and haven't spoken to one another in years, but she did send flowers to Aaron's funeral. Yeah, come to think of it...there is someone I could ask."

J.J. tried to think. Then, it hit him. Oh no, he thought. Not that.

"No way." J.J. muttered.

Selma replied, "Yes sir! Now hush, Officer James and I are talking."

Steve said, "You have someone in mind?"

"Yes. I can have him stay with my sister Doris while I'm at work," said Selma.

Steve smiled. He patted J.J. on the back. "Terrific," he said, "as long as you've got it figured out, I will release him to your custody. I need to get out there on the streets again."

Selma said, "Thanks, Officer James. See you at church this weekend?"

Steve smiled and nodded. He waved goodbye and left the bookstore. J.J. sighed. Now, he knew he was in trouble. Bad.

"Mom," he whined.

"Hush, child. Darling, I know this is hard. it is killing me inside, too. Your father would not have wanted you to keep up with such company. He would have wanted you to-"

This time, it was J.J.'s turn to break down and cry. His mom hugged J.J. She rocked him gently.

"I'm sorry, Mamma. I can be good. Please. Just give me another chance," J.J. said.

"Baby, you know I would. But, you are headed down the wrong path. Those boys. They can just lead you to jail. Or dead. I love you too much to let that happen. Not when we have choices we can make. Now, let's call Aunt Doris," Selma reassured.

"But mom," J.J. objected.

"What's that, child?" Selma said.

"Aunt Doris is a witch."

The kitchen was lined with herbs and spices, dried and bottled. A middle-aged Haitian woman stirred a steaming pot on a cast iron, wooden stove. A black cat meowed contentedly. She reached down and picked up the animal.

"Now, don't you fret, Lando. They will be here soon. Wonders never cease, Lando. I guess we all get second...sometimes even third and fourth chances. Now get. Go chase some mice or something. Make yourself useful," Aunt Doris said, setting down her pet.

Aunt Doris, hunchback from osteoporosis, continued to stir the mysterious contents of the pot. The front doorbell rang. She smiled, revealing ragged, yellowy teeth. One eye was partially covered in a milky cateract, the other looked sideways in lazy fashion.

Aunt Doris opened the door. Selma and J.J. stood in the hall, both looked pained and slightly ashamed. "Ain't you two a sight?" Doris said.

"Aunt Doris. It's been so long," Selma said.

"Too long. Now, this strapping young man must be J.J. Come on in, you two," Aunt Doris invited.

"J.J.," Selma said, "say hello to your great Aunt Doris."

"Hello, Aunt Doris." J.J. parroted.

Doris scoffed. "Son, you goin' to have to do better than that."

She held out her hands, expecting a hug. J.J. looked at his mother. Selma nodded, meaning "if you know what is best for you". J.J. hugged her. Aunt Doris smelled funny.

Aunt Doris hugged back firmly, rocking J.J. like his mother sometimes did. "Yeah, we goin' to get along just fine, ain't we?"

"Yes, ma'am."

Doris cackled. "Well, I see your mom been raising you with manners. That's something."

Selma interjected, "J.J. is a good boy, Aunt Doris. He's just fell in with the wrong bunch of boys is all."

"Oh, I know he is. I can just tell. Just like you were a good girl, Sel. Still, good ones still get lost from time to time. That's why the good Lord invented second chances," Aunt Doris proclaimed.

"Yes, ma'am," Selma echoed.

"Speaking of second chances, I want to thank you for giving me one, Sel. I know we ain't always seen eye to eye on things, but it is mighty Christian of you to forgive and forget," Aunt Doris said sheepishly.

Selma looked incredulously at Aunt Doris. Her mouth hung slightly ajar. "Aunt Doris, I should be thanking you for the second chance. I screwed up and I am sorry."

Aunt Doris laughed. "This is funny. I have heard of forgive and forget, but never forget who forgives!"

Selma laughed. J.J. looked around, not knowing what to do with his arms. They felt awkward and he kept changing them, crossing and then letting them hang limply at his sides. They felt alien to him, as if they were not his arms at all.

A lithe black cat rubbed at J.J.'s feet. It purred, begging to be picked up. J.J. looked up at his mother. "Mom, I can't be around cats. I'm allergic."

Selma winced, smiling but her eyes looked helpless. "Little old Lando here? Lando never hurt no body. Did you, Lando?"

Selma said, "We just have to do our best, honey. Wash your face and hands a lot. Try not to touch the cat. You should be fine."

Aunt Doris replied, "Yeah, don't you fret none, child. I'll take care of you. I can whip up some of my famous herbal tea. I got a batch that can cure a head cold. Maybe I can tweak it a bit for allergies."

Selma smiled, "That sounds great. Doesn't it, J.J.?"

J.J. shrugged.

"I'm sorry I have to just say hello and run, but I have to get to work. I am over on my break now as it is. Going to be on thin ice if I ain't careful," Selma said.

"Think nothing of it, Sel. Run along. J.J. and I are going to have lots of fun," Aunt Doris said, smiling.

After a bit, J.J. realized how difficult this was going to be. He might as well be home alone, like before. Aunt Doris had been in the kitchen all day.

There was no television in her house. There were no games. No toys, even. An old rocking chair and leather ottoman were the only pieces of furniture in the living room. Several old artifacts and primitive looking artwork and sculptures made up the decor. Bookshelves lined the walls.

J.J. picked out a book from a shelf, thumbing through it. He must be getting desperate for entertainment, he mused. The book, though, was written in French. There were weird symbols throughout under the unknown words. J.J. replaced the book on the shelf.

"You speak French, Aunt Doris?" he called out.

Aunt Doris yelled back, "Why, child? You need help in school?"

"Nevermind."

J.J. walked aimlessly around the place, winding up in the hallway. A hall closet door was to his left. Without thinking, J.J. reached for the handle and began to turn it.

A gnarled old hand seized his arm, squeezing firmly. J.J. cried out in surprise and slight pain. He turned to face Aunt Doris. Her brow furrowed in anger and her mouth was etched in a scowl.

Aunt Doris pulled J.J.'s arm back, still holding it firmly. She had quite the grip for an old lady, J.J. thought. He winced.

Aunt Doris spoke slowly and with conviction, her thick Cajun accent all but disappearing. She said, "Now, you keep to yourself and we'll get along fine. I don't want you snooping around, though. This especially applies to this here hall closet. It is at the top of the list of things you best stay out of. Got it? Touch anything you want in the living room, but you keep your mitts off this hall closet."

J.J. nodded his head, whimpering slightly. Aunt Doris looked down at his arm. Her grip had made an impression of ghostly fingers on his arm. She released it. Her face softened, and she let out a nervous laugh.

"I'm sorry there, boy. I hope you know that your Great Ole Auntie can be a bit rough around the edges from time to time. She don't mean no harm, though. Just that I been under a little stress lately. Oh, not you or your mom. Not that. Something else I'm doing. Your mom tell you what I got going on?" Aunt Doris asked.

J.J. shook his head. Aunt Doris lead him into the kitchen, her twisted finger beckoning for him to follow. He obliged, not knowing what else to do.

The kitchen was overwrought with what seemed to be a mish-mash of cooking equipment and materials. There were pots, pans, spices, and all sorts of raw materials strewn about. It was a cacophony of culinary disaster. Or so it seemed to J.J.

Aunt Doris waved a hand at the mess proudly. She said, "I got my own catering business, son. It's just now starting to take off too, which can account for the disarray of things. That's my problem. Business has grown so much, I am floundering like a catfish on the line. What I could really use is some help. You want to help your Aunt Doris?"

J.J. smirked. He shrugged his shoulders. Aunt Doris took that as a yes and said, "Good. J.J., look. I know your mama and you been through a lot lately. It's tough. That's one reason why I never married. That and the fact that I am uglier than what gets scraped out of Lando's catbox."

Aunt Doris snorted heartily. J.J. tried to smile, but wound up wincing again. She was loud and it hurt his ears.

She picked up a bowl of raw shrimp from the counter. Aunt Doris thrust it at J.J. When he wouldn't take it, she nodded. Finally, he grabbed it.

"I need these shelled and de-veined, boy," she ordered.

J.J. grabbed a shrimp and tried to figure out what to do with it. He looked at Aunt Doris, but she gave no indication that she was going to help. He wound up pulling one apart and in pieces, clumsily.

Aunt Doris took it from him and threw it in the trash. "Try again," she said.

J.J. grabbed another shrimp. He crushed it like someone trying to peel an egg with a hammer. "This is hard. I don't want to do it," he objected.

Aunt Doris grabbed the squashed shrimp and threw it in the garbage. She set the bowl on the counter, and pulled J.J. up alongside her. "Not all things that need done come easy," she said.

J.J. watched as his great aunt took a shrimp out of the bowl. With a single flick of her arthritic fingers, she flung the shell off the shrimp and tossed it in the trash in one piece. Then, she grabbed a small knife and spun it along the back of the shrimp. She quickly pulled out what looked like a little black earthworm and threw it away, as well.

"See, I told you. Nothing to it, J.J. We just need someone to show us how it is done," she instructed.

J.J. got some practice, and after about a half dozen mistakes he got one right. He cried out, triumphantly. He showed Aunt Doris his accomplishment.

Aunt Doris beamed. She smiled, and took it from him. She put it on a large metal cooking sheet and spread it apart. "Now, we just have three or four hundred more to go, child," she cackled.

Despite himself, J.J. found that he was enjoying preparing shrimp with his Aunt Doris. He felt pride at being good at something.

"Yeah, this ain't so bad," he said under his breath.

From the corner of his eye, he saw Aunt Doris nodding her head. She began to hum, contentedly. J.J. smiled.

"Hey, Aunt Doris, why you got so many weird things in this place?" he asked.

She laughed. "Fish gotta swim, J.J. fish gotta swim."

It was all the answer he was going to get, so J.J. let it be. He continued to peel and de-vein shrimp. Aunt Doris went over to the large pot on the stove and added ingredients. She took a wooden spoon and dipped it in the broth, bringing it to her wrinkly lips. She sucked it in, frowning.

"Curse it," she spat.

"What's that, Aunt Doris?"

"I'm kind of like Beethoven," she replied.

J.J. asked, "What's in the oven?"

"Not in the oven. Beethoven. He was a composer from long ago, child," Aunt Doris explained.

"Was he a friend of yours?" asked J.J.

Aunt Doris laughed again, this time until she cried. She snorted and said, "I ain't that old, J.J. Close, but not that old. I got a Great Aunt of my own might be closer. She practices spells and such in the bayou. Works for baubles in an old shack in the middle of the swamp. Even has an alligator for a pet, if you can believe that. But Beethoven, child. He wrote beautiful music. Hold on, I'll show you."

Aunt Doris wiped her hands on a dish towel and left momentarily. J.J. continued to work on the task at hand. Shortly, a bouncy wordless little piano song emanated through the small house. J.J. grinned.

Aunt Doris returned. "Beethoven. This one is called Für Elise."

J.J. added, "It's good for peeling shrimp, all right."

"You're a great help, J.J. Thank you." Aunt Doris said.

J.J. welled with satisfaction. He was unexpectedly happy.

"Funny thing here, J.J. Beethoven was terrific, but he went deaf as a post. He wrote music from memory. Couldn't hear a note of his own symphonies." Aunt Doris explained.

"Wow." J.J. commented.

"Now, I am kind of like that. No, I ain't ready to sit at the same table with Beethoven. But I can't cook as well as I used to. Lost my tasters," Aunt Doris stated.

Aunt Doris grabbed the spoon and scooped it in the pot. She walked towards J.J. "I can cook up some great recipes my mama taught me, but I can't tell how they turned out. Can you help me, J.J.?"

She thrust the spoon towards J.J. Suddenly, he felt uncomfortable. "I'm just a kid. I don't know nothin'," he said.

"Nonsense," she said, "your tasters are still fresh. Young. I bet you got great tasters, just never used 'em. Too busy filling them them cheese puffs and sugar candy."

J.J. looked at the broth in the spoon. Tendrils of steam wafted upwards. Aunt Doris blew it off. She pushed it towards his lips.

Reluctantly, J.J. sipped the broth. It was spicy. "Hot. Burning my tongue," he said.

"But good?" Aunt Doris probed.

J.J. nodded.

"That's good. Just how it should be. I got a southern wedding coming up. They want authentic Louisiana cooking. That's what I do best," she said.

A slower, more somber tune came on replacing the bouncy lighter song. J.J. felt his tongue swelling. He grew dizzy. The song grew more and more ominous.

"Moonlight Sonata. This is not as good if you are trying to get through a lot of work," Aunt Doris explained.

J.J.'s feet felt strange. His brow began to sweat. The music gave him the impression everything was going in slow motion. His knees buckled.

His eyes rolled back as J.J. fell to the floor. He dropped a shrimp on the ground. The room went black. He began convulsing, foam bubbling in his mouth. Lando hissed at him. The cat ran to the shrimp and snatched it, tearing off with his ill-gotten prize to some unseen corner of the house.

J.J. began to twich. His heart beat furiously in his chest. His throat closed. He was dying.

Aunt Doris called for help.

The ambulance arrived as quickly as they could. The paramedics worked on the small boy. A plastic tube was thrust down his closed throat. They pumped air into J.J's lungs with a bag.

Another paramedic began compressions on the boy's chest. The defibrillator whined with a high pitch, indicating it was ready. The paramedic cut the boy's "Mario Brothers" shirt with crooked scissors.

"Clear!" a paramedic shouted.

The other man removed his hands from the bag. The paramedic put the paddles of the defibrillator against the boys chest and ribs. The boy jolted with the shock.

The paramedic listened with a stethoscope. He shook his head and repeated the treatment. The boy bucked violently. The other paramedic felt for a heartbeat. He shook his head. The paramedic tried a third time, shocking the small child's bare chest.

At the hospital, Selma ran to Aunt Doris. The old woman was waiting in the lobby, her eyes distant and worried. Selma hugged her. The women cried, holding one another tightly.

A door opened, and a short little bald man walked out. He was the emergency doctor on call that helped J.J. Aunt Doris saw his grim expression and wailed.

"Oh, God! Please, not again, God. Please, Not J.J. Not little J.J.!" Selma pleaded.

"Mrs. Johnston. Please, Mrs. Johnston," the doctor said.

"Why? Why?" Selma asked.

"Mrs. Johnston. We managed to revive J.J. He has come through the worst of it, but he isn't out of the woods quite yet," the doctor explained.

Selma laughed. Aunt Doris smiled, rubbing her back. "May I ask you some questions?" the doctor said.

"About?" Selma asked.

The doctor said, "Is J.J. allergic to anything?"

"Cats," Selma stated.

"No," the doctor replied, "any food allergies? We believe J.J. went into anaphylactic shock from something he ate."

Selma looked at Aunt Doris.

The hospital room was okay. People brought J.J. drinks. He had a remote to the TV set. He even liked the nurse. He just felt like a car had run him over, then backed up just to make sure.

Selma and Aunt Doris came in the room. J.J. could tell his mother had been crying. Her eyes were puffy and swollen. Aunt Doris looked like a dog who'd gotten into the garbage.

"Oh, baby. I was so worried. How are you, honey?" Selma asked.

J.J. was surprised to hear his voice. It was raspy and sounded more like Aunt Doris' voice than his own. "I'm okay, I guess. What happened?"

"Scallops," Selma replied.

"What?"

"You are deathly allergic to scallops. We almost lost you, baby," Selma said, tears welling in her eyes.

J.J. asked, "What are scallops?"

"Seafood," Selma stated.

Aunt Doris lifted her head, but could not make eye contact with J.J. She said, "It was in that stock you tasted, Little Man."

J.J. looked at his Aunt Doris. Now, he understood. He remembered. "You...you tried to kill me," he exclaimed.

Aunt Doris recoiled as if slapped. "Oh, baby child, no. No no no. I would never do that. I've done a lot of rotten things in my life, and had more than my fair share of second chances, but hurting my sweet little grand-nephew ain't on that list."

"J.J., nobody knew you were allergic to scallops. You don't like seafood, and we usually don't have the budget for such things. We just didn't know," Selma said.

Aunt Doris walked closer to the bed. J.J. winced, shrinking back as far as he could. She stopped advancing.

Selma said, "Maybe you had better wait outside, Aunt Doris. I will straighten this all out. No worries."

Aunt Doris nodded. "I'd never hurt you, J.J. Promise. I'm sorry. So sorry."

And with that she left the hospital room. Selma knelt down, sitting on the corner of the bed. She smiled at her son.

"Baby, she didn't know. Really. It's not her fault. In life, we have to give people second chances. Or more. Your mama has made some bad choices. Aunt Doris let that be swept under the rug and opened her home to us. You need to let this be water under the bridge and forgive, sweety," Selma said, soothingly.

J.J. frowned. His mother didn't care. She didn't understand. "Why should it matter what she thinks, anyway? What about what I think. I am the one who almost died," he said.

"Give her another chance, J.J. It was just an accident. We need to get over this. It does matter what you think, but there is some other stuff you don't know about. Things are a little different now. We need Aunt Doris in our lives," Selma pleaded.

J.J. scowled. "Why? Why should we?"

Selma explained, "You know we've been through some hard times. Your dad was always there for us. He's not here, now. I know it hurts. It hurts bad. But things are going to be a lot different when you get out of here, Honey."

"What's changing? I don't understand," J.J. said.

"J.J., Honey. Baby. I am so sorry, but we have to move."

"Move? You mean out of the house?"

"Yes. I can't afford it with your daddy gone. And now, it's even worse because..." Selma paused.

"What?" J.J. prompted.

"Now, J.J. This ain't your fault. And it ain't Aunt Doris' fault. It's just life. Don't blame anyone, okay?" Selma began.

"Mom, tell me!" J.J. said.

Selma stated, "It's just that the bookstore wouldn't let me take any more time off. I used up all my allowances when your father died. Now, I couldn't let my baby stay in the hospital without being nearby in case anything happened, could I?"

"Oh, mom! What are we going to do?" J.J. asked.

Selma said, "That's just what I am trying to tell you. The bills for all this doctor stuff are incredible. I have to sell the house and our car just to-"

"Our car? House?" J.J. whined.

"Yes, baby, and most of our furniture and stuff. We won't have room for it anyway. J.J., Aunt Doris asked us to live with her...and I have accepted," Selma revealed.

"Mom!"

"It won't be that bad. I can help her out with the catering...we both can. Aunt Doris says that you are a whiz at-"

"But Aunt Doris? She tried to kill me!" J.J. argued.

"No she didn't, honey."

"And the cat," J.J. faught, "I am so allergic to it. And the place is small, even for one person, and-"

"J.J., you don't understand," Selma sighed.

"Mom, no."

"J.J., ain't I always straight with you? This is no different, Baby. This is going to cost us for a long time. Our insurance won't make a dent. We do not have any other choice. I just thank God that we even have an Aunt Doris to run to. What if we didn't, baby? Think about that," Selma explained.

After J.J. recovered for a while in the hospital, he came to live in his great Aunt Doris' house. Selma had already made up a corner of her room as his, since the house only had two bedrooms. He had to share with his mom. He supposed it was better than living in a shelter somewhere. Or on the streets.

Aunt Doris and Selma had already gotten into a routine. They cooked and made catering orders. Selma even suggested they branch out and do event coordination. Wedding planning. Aunt Doris wanted to catch up on the catering orders she was already doing, though, and said they would talk more about it later.

J.J. tried to find his place. He didn't know what to think. Late one night, he lay awake in bed. His mom was out like a light, snoring soundly. J.J. remembered the hall closet.

J.J. sat up, sneaking past his mother. He creaked open the door. Selma rolled over, but did not wake.

The house was dark in the wake of a moonless night. J.J. had to feel along the hallway until he came across the closet door. His heart began to beat angrily in his chest. He swallowed.

J.J. felt his arm reach out in the darkness. His fingers wriggled until the came across the door handle. He tightened his grasp. Slowly, he turned the handle.

J.J. heard a click, and opened the door just a crack. From behind him, a loud hiss startled the boy. He gasped, then realized it was just Lando.

"Shut up, you old mangy cat," he whispered.

J.J. opened the door a little more. He could not see anything, and the closet was no exception. Instead, he felt around.

There were no towels or old clothes. His hands ran across something cold and clammy. Something that felt slightly damp. Try as he might, his brain could not imagine what it might be.

J.J. had to risk turning on a light. He felt around, knowing the closet in his bedroom had a pull string for a single hanging bulb. Sure enough, this closet had a similar lighting feature. J.J. yanked the cord.

The small space instantly filled with a yellow light. J.J. looked at what he had felt. He quit breathing, eyes widening.

A corpse hung neatly in the closet. It was mostly skeletal, with a few sinewy strands of tissue remaining. J.J. backed up, terrified.

He ran into Aunt Doris, who flung a gnarled hand over his mouth to stop the boy from screaming. Her grip was firm so J.J. didn't struggle.

"Thought I told you not to mess around in here, boy? Well, now you know," Aunt Doris whispered.

The cat hissed at her feet. "Hush, Lando. Now, J.J. Don't judge. We all have a skeleton or two in the closet. Mine just has a little more meat on it," Aunt Doris whispered.

Aunt Doris lowered her hand from over J.J.'s mouth. She stepped back, smiling. J.J. stood motionless and looked at her with large eyes.

"Now, J.J., you forgave me once about the scallops. Can't you give me another chance and forget about this too?"

J.J. nodded. What other choice did he have? Aunt Doris patted him on the back, and J.J. went back to bed.

In the morning, the three of them peeled and de-veined shrimp. J.J. was good at it. He looked up from his work and caught Aunt Doris' eye. She winked at him. J.J. smiled back.

## THE WARLOCK'S GARDEN

### *October Sixth*

Dolnak the Conqueror had gotten old, even by Warlock standards. It was nigh time for him to retire. So, he did.

He found a small corner of the forbidden forest to call his own. He set up a small shack and prepared to live the rest of his days in relaxing solitude.

He grew bored. Dolnak was used to mighty wars and casting spells. Sitting back and watching the toadstools grow was dull.

His friend, Porcella the witch, came by to visit. Since losing her sisters, she sought his company. He never really thought much of her before. Now that he was retired, their afternoon tea was a highlight of his day.

"Why don't you find yourself a nice hobby?" Porcella suggested.

She took her hook and scratched the wart on the side of her nose. Dolnak thought she looked more like a pirate than a witch with her missing hand and leg, but he would never tell Porcella as much. She had been through enough already. What made matters worse was that she had lost her wand waving hand. Dolnak shuddered at the thought.

"What would I do?" Dolnak asked.

"Gardening is always nice," said Porcella.

So, Dolnak figured he would try. He had nothing but time to kill, anyway. Soon, he had a garden outside his shack.

Porcella had to attend to affairs on the eastern lands, so Dolnak didn't see her for many a season. In the meantime, he had gotten quite adept at gardening. He couldn't wait to show Porcella.

Upon her return, she paid him a visit.

Dolnak was proud as everything looked perfect. Porcella gave him a sideways glance. "Are you sure you've retired?"

"Why do you ask?"

Porcella looked at his garden. Vegetation sprouted from human skulls made into planters. He was growing wolfsbane, death fruit, and nightshade. "Your garden looks like a working witch's pantry."

"Well, I just stuck with what I knew. Still retired. I haven't cast a spell in ages."

"What about the skulls?" Porcella asked.

"Oh, I acquired those the old fashioned way. No magic. I promise."

"Good, deary. Now how about showing some hospitality for an old friend?"

They went inside for tea.

# FINISH THE STORY, GRANDPA

*October Seventh*

"Read it again, Grandpa," Marcus said.

Emily nodded enthusiastically. "Yes, Um-pah."

Grandpa smiled, milking every ounce of attention he could get. The eldest, Samantha, hadn't chimed in. She was eight and getting too old for stories. Still, she glanced at her grandfather sideways in anticipation.

"Would you like to hear it to, Sam?" he asked.

"I suppose," she whispered.

"Ok, then. It is a consensus," Grandpa said.

"Not the senses one, read the dragon one," Emily protested.

"Of course, little Em. Now, I can only start this story if I can finish it. If I don't, the creature will escape. If that happens, well…I sure wouldn't want to be around," Grandpa began.

"Yes, yes yes," Marcus beamed.

Grandpa took out the storybook. The children huddled around. He started reading, "The Sapphire Palm Dragon. Once upon a time there was a princess with a very warm heart. The kingdom had been plagued by dragons, which had destroyed the crops of the village and burned down most of the houses. The castle was the last refuge. A handsome king declared war on the beasts. Many on both sides perished in conflicts.

"It filled the princess with despair to see such amazing creatures as the dragons destroyed. Soon, they would be wiped out entirely. She grew despondent, begging her father not to eradicate all the dragons.

"Having compassion for his daughter, and adoring her gentle heart, he agreed to save the last dragon. It was a small dragon of a deep blue hue. The creature had been captured in a glass bottle, which easily fit in the palm of the king's hand.

"Knowing that the dragon would grow and be a threat, the king decided to imprison the sapphire palm dragon in the pages of a storybook. This very book that you are holding. In that fashion, the creature would be forever--"

Grandpa held his left arm, dropping the book. He keeled over.

"Grandpa!" they shouted.

They took him in an ambulance amidst the crying of inconsolable children. In all the raucous, nobody noticed the small blue dragon as it emerged from the ornately illustrated book. That would soon change, however, as the dragon began to grow.

# SHAPESHIFTER

## *October Eighth*

The night was cool, but not as much as it should have been for this time of year. Old Man Winter was already sneaking his presence in early autumn. It was too cold too early in the season. Akecheta breathed in the frigid night air deeply to calm his nerves.

The reservation was in the wastelands of Arizona, between Page and Flagstaff and little else in between. Sometimes, when things got tough, they made a trek into a small Native American town called Cameron. Mostly, they were off the beaten path and on their own. A tribe within a tribe. Separated by more than geography.

Even so, none of their remaining thirteen members were willing to leave the tribe. They all had a blood oath to see the battle through. They were being hunted and had to band together to survive.

Once, they had been a small tribe in the fifties. Over the years, that had dwindled to the mere teens.

"Soon, it will come. The winds tell me," said Cha'kwaina.

The old woman's blind eyes looked out past Akecheta. She was the secret weapon. She knew when a shapeshifter was on the hunt. And tonight, the hunter would become the hunted.

The old woman had only been used for defense before. But now, Akecheta brought Ogaleesha and Wakiza with him tonight in the hopes of killing the shapeshifter. They brought their sacred daggers. It was to be an ambush.

The four of them sat on the rocks outside of the main road near the gas station. Though the lands were flat and the shapeshifters could attack from anywhere, Cha'kwaina had told them the shifter would come that way. So, they waited.

It didn't take long. Soon, a man rode in on a motorcycle. He parked next to the pumps and went into the small store.

"What if he is only a man?" Ogaleesha asked.

"Then it would be murder," Wakiza replied.

The three warriors drew their knives and went after the man inside the small store. Cha'kwaina cocked her head listening. She never saw the motorcycle transform into a woman who stalked her quietly. A woman with very long fingernails and sharp, protruding teeth.

# CURSE OF WINGATE MANSION

## *October Ninth*

Sondra Levy walked through the woodlands. Horace, her cameraman, struggled to keep her in frame as he wrestled with various equipment. Dusk approached, so Horace turned on the lighting so as not to lose the reporter in the impending gloom.

Sondra narrated, "Arguably, one of the most infamous serial killers of the last century is Gaines Roland Pickett. These woods were the burial ground for thirteen of his known victims.

"Gaines believed that through these crimes, he would achieve immortality. He buried their dismembered corpses in shallow graves on this very path.

"Their blood soaked the ground and fed these trees. Trees that were later used to build Wingate Mansion."

Horace let Sondra walk out of frame for dramatic effect. "Beautiful, Sondra," he said.

Sondra walked back, beaming. "I know this is fluff filler, but I am really enjoying it."

"Too bad it wasn't a live remote," Horace commented.

Sondra nodded. "We'll run it in segments with lead promos. I'll make a name for us both, Horace."

"Well, at least we didn't have to be war correspondents to do so. I would rather deal with dead spooks than live ammunition."

"Not me. I would do anything. Part of the reason I became a reporter was because of my insatiable curiosity."

Horace nodded in agreement. Had Sondra been a cat, she would have perished a long time ago.

Horace said, "I just want to get another shot of the woods while the lighting is good. Should look really spooky with the sun shining through. It makes the Spanish moss glow ever so eerily, too."

Horace set up the tripod and mounted the camera. He hit record and did a slow pan through the forest. The surroundings were unnerving.

Horace gathered his equipment. They hiked towards the mansion. "You know, I'm not filming now. You could help me carry some of this crap," he said.

She replied, "I could, but then I would be breaking O.S.H.A. laws."

"Nice out."

She smiled. "I thought so."

The two approached the large Victorian mansion. It loomed over them. The place was in shambles, desperately in need of repair. Old paint crinkled and curled from its sides. The rickety shudders barely hung from rusty hinges. The shingles on the roof had shed in places like scales off of an old snake. Horace filmed an establishing shot.

Inside, cobwebs hung from everything and dust coated the place. Nobody had been inside for years. Antique furniture and paintings still adorned the interior. Even an old grandfather clock stood silently in the corner. Thieves had not looted the place for fear of supernatural retribution.

The floorboards creaked with every step. They surveyed the place for the best background. The main foyer dripped with atmosphere, so they chose it.

While Horace set up the lighting and camera, Sondra ran through her lines. After a moment, they were both ready for the next segment.

Horace began filming. Sondra continued, "Philip Wingate had a taste for the macabre. Wingate purchased these woods after Pickett was hanged. Wingate consigned laborers to complete this mansion from the timber.

"From that point on, death has plagued Wingate Mansion. Four workers perished while pouring the basement. Their skeletal remains are permanently embedded in the concrete.

"Alice Wingate gave birth here, but her child was stillborn. Three days later, Philip found her lifeless corpse hanging from the banister of the spiral staircase to my left.

"Philip grew insane with grief. He told tales of the ghost of Gaines Roland Pickett cursing Wingate Mansion. The ghost informed him that the blood of the thirteenth victim would spill on the wood of the place and bring it to life.

"Philip Wingate himself became the seventh victim. He tried to break the curse by setting the mansion afire. Mysteriously, the doors of his bedroom slammed and locked shut, effectively containing the fire that consumed Philip but little else.

"With no heirs, the mansion became property of the state. While attempting to bring the place up to current code, five workers lost their lives when a seemingly new and safe water heater violently exploded.

"That brings the curse up to twelve. Gretta and Igna Solfern have since purchased Wingate Mansion with the purpose of turning it into a bed and breakfast. The Solferns have given us permission to spend the night in Wingate Mansion. We'll keep you posted on all the 'things that go bump in the night'. Sondra Levy, Channel Four News."

Horace cut the tape, smiling. "First take, Sondra. You're a real pro! I told you we should have been live."

"Thanks, Horace."

"Where now?" he asked.

"I was thinking we would get a POV shot from the top of the staircase."

"Good idea," Horace replied.

With that, they made the trek upstairs. The floors continued to protest their movement. The creaks echoed through the cavernous rooms.

Horace set up from the top of the stairwell. The grandfather clock began to chime downstairs. "Guess it still works, huh?"

The chimes grew louder, echoing ominously up towards them. Five, six chimes. With every gong, Sondra grew more anxious. Horace leaned over the railing, adjusting the equipment. Eight, nine chimes.

Horace turned around. Ten, Eleven. "Hurry up, maybe we can get some audio of that clock." Horace said.

Sondra violently pushed Horace. She saw his eyes widen and his arms flailed out, desperately trying to grasp something to break his fall. Nothing did. Twelve chimes.

Horace plummeted down, smacking brutally on the hard wood floor. Sondra held her breath. She knew she was too curious for her own good.

"I told you I would make a name for us." she called out.

The grandfather clocked chimed again. Thirteen.

Blood ran from Horace's lifeless eyes and mouth. It trickled down to the floor, dripping in earnest.

The wooden slats of the floor soaked up the blood like a sponge. A deep, animal-like growl emanated through the mansion. It was followed by a maniacal laugh.

Upstairs, Sondra gasped in terror. "What would happen to the fourteenth victim?" she wondered.

At least she knew her curiosity would finally be sated.

# WHAT ALES YOU

## *October Tenth*

Witches have been around since Biblical times. Evil since the Garden of Eden. The concept of what a witch make look like, however, has only been around since the middle ages.

What image comes to mind when you think of the stereotypical witch? An old hag carrying a long wooden broomstick. She wears a dark hood or cloak. A pointed hat sits atop her head. A witch tends a bubbling caldron with a black cat at the ready. Her shelves are lined with herbs, ingredients, and a book of spells.

Would it surprise you to know that this description is part of a conspiracy to usurp a thriving commercial model? That everything you think about a witch in the classical sense is due to propaganda used in a hostile business takeover? The image of witches was a smear campaign.

In less enlightened times, women were thought of as considerably less value than men. They were charged with menial labor such as cleaning, laundry, tending gardens, and preparing meals. Part of cooking was providing drink. Beer was a staple since it was safer to drink than water.

Many men, on the other hand, were out with conquest often for extended periods of time. This left women as the sole providers. They put their children in charge of the household chores. The women banded together to sell the only marketable product they knew how to make – beer.

Breweries were formed. Production was increased substantially. The alehouses needed to move product and get the word out. They needed marketing.

Alewives began to dress the same so they would be easily recognizable. This included a long pointed hat and carrying around a broom. Two unmistakable signs that the woman was an alewife and could sell you beer.

Beer was brewed in large black cauldrons. Alewives kept cats to protect the grains they needed to brew beer. Recipe books kept the product consistent.

It was big business. Too big. Soon, men in power realized that this wasn't simply women's work. This was a thriving enterprise.

A scheme was born. One to vilify the alewives and steal their business. One that would remain in place to this day.

And it worked.

# SPOILED

*October Eleventh*

Angst, Rolette, and Porcella bickered, as usual. It was a wonder they had been able to work together in the first place to capture the little brats. But they had.

And brats they were. They didn't even have the courtesy to realize their predicament. After they had been lured into the cottage to pet their black cat Witten, the three witches seized the children. They hadn't even cried out. They merely acted like it was all some sort of game.

"We need to tenderize them," Porcella suggested.

Angst shook her head, scratching the coarse stubbly white hairs on her chin. Her long nose furrowed. "No, you cow. They're young. Their meat is tender already. If we do anything to it, it is likely to fall apart."

"I like meat that falls off the bone," said Rolette.

"Nobody asked you," Angst scolded.

The children played some sort of game. They clapped each other's hands. The siblings just didn't get that they were about to be devoured by hungry witches.

Angst smiled, rotting teeth protruding at odd angles. She could smell her own fowl breath and decided to use it. She walked over to the cage made from stolen cemetery fence posts. The two children looked up at her.

"I say we boil them alive. Their agonized screams will be our appetizer. Our mouths will water as their eyeballs harden and their hair cooks off. Their entrails will be nice and tasty by that time," Angst said with a cackle.

Rolette and Porcella clapped and cheered.

Aside from the boy grabbing his nose in disgust, there was no other reaction from the children. Perhaps they didn't speak the queen's tongue, she thought. Maybe they couldn't understand what they were saying at all.

That was no fun.

"Do you understand what we are saying?" Angst asked.

"Yes," replied the girl.

"Aren't you afraid?" Porcella asked.

They shook their heads 'no'.

"Why not?" asked Rolette.

"All we need to do is whistle," said the boy.

"Whistle?" Angst asked.

"Yeah, like this," he said.

The two whistled in unison. Immediately, the door crashed and split. A very large man with a very large axe burst in.

Their meal was spoiled.

# UNREAL ESTATE

### *October Twelfth*

"You must be the Coulters. Come in, let me show you around," said the woman in the lavender dress.

"I'm Floyd and this is Val," Floyd said.

"Don't you just love it? I can't get over how much the place has changed," the real estate agent said.

Then, she pulled something out of her pocket. It was a small lollipop. She unwrapped it and put it in her mouth. "Oh, this," she said, "I thought I should give up smoking. This is supposed to help. Plus, they are tasty. Do you want one?"

Val and Floyd both politely declined. They followed the woman into the house. The interior was beautiful.

"Of course, it has all been redone since the fire. The only reason it is so inexpensive is local sentiment," she said.

"What do you mean?" Val asked.

"You haven't heard of the ghost, then?" asked the woman.

Floyd and Val laughed. The agent didn't smile. "You're serious?" Floyd said.

"Very. Folks in small towns, you know. They say that after the fire, you can still see the lady of the house in the upstairs room. They say she pounds at the window screaming for help as ghostly flames devour her," she said.

"So, she died in the fire upstairs?" Val asked.

The woman shrugged. "Yes," she said, "but you know small towns. Gossip and local lore. The place has been entirely redone since then.

It's a steal for what they are asking. Enlightened folks like yourself need not worry about superstition like that."

After the tour, the Coulters walked out to their car waving their goodbyes. As they turned to leave, a car pulled up beside them. Out fumbled a strange little man with a bowtie.

"Oh, wonderful, you haven't left. Are you ready to see the house?" he asked.

"Who are you?" Val asked.

"Oh, my apologies. I am Gilbert, the real estate agent. Now, in full disclosure, I have to tell you that there was a fire in the building. Quite sad. A young woman fell asleep smoking," he said.

Floyd looked down. A blue lollipop wrapper twisted about on the ground. It blew away with a sudden, cold gust of wind.

## CHALKMAN

### *October Thirteenth*

It was a sunny autumn day. Usually, the children outside playing would have made her smile. For some reasons, they congregated outside her front yard. Today they were drawing on her sidewalk in multi-colored pastel chalk.

Marybeth considered telling them to go away because she had a headache. She feared, however, that they would not return. She just wanted them to go away for today.

Maybe if she turned the sprinklers on "accidentally" they would run off and come back later. She giggled at the thought. Sure, it was a bit mean, but she was feeling a touch mean.

She snuck past the living room window, hoping she wasn't observed from outside. She went to the hall and opened the closet. The maintenance men had installed the control box in there as the wiring came through the garage.

Marybeth turned the front zone to manual and hit on. She heard children screaming in chaos. She peeked out the window again. The kids were grabbing their sticks of chalk and running. All but one child, who had her back to Marybeth.

The young girl was wearing a blue dress. It was getting wet, but the kid didn't seem to notice. She continued to draw on the sidewalk. The water drenched her and the back of her hair.

Feeling guilty, Marybeth turned off the water. She grabbed a towel and went out to the child. "Sorry, honey, the sprinklers just came on," she lied.

Marybeth placed the towel around the child. She looked up and Marybeth gasped. She must have been an albino or something because her skin was so white. And her eyes. They were all black.

"Chalkman is going to get you," whispered the child.

Marybeth looked at the sidewalk. The child had protected the drawing from water. It was a man with a long knife. It appeared to be stabbing the other children's drawings. Because of the water washing part of them away, they looked like they were bleeding.

Marybeth went back to the house. She left the towel around the child. She closed the front door.

On the back of the door was a life-size drawing of the Chalkman. It smiled at her.

# DEATH PACT

### *October Fourteenth*

Nina, Adele, Priscilla, and Levina were fixtures at the community center every Saturday night. Even when Adele's husband, Seymour, died - they only missed one week. They had been meeting together to play "pitch" for almost thirty years, after all.

Each took turns bringing the snacks. The employees at the check in counter made exceptions for the ladies since, technically, they predated the "no food in the gym" rule. Also, because they had been steady customers for more than most of them had been alive.

This week was Levina's turn, which meant Nina would be unhappy. Levina loved cheese and usually used it liberally in her creations. Nina was lactose intolerant, a fact which seemed to perpetually elude poor Levina's memory. Usually, either Adele or Priscilla brought a little something for Nina, so it all worked out.

The group arrived at five in their usual fashion that Saturday night. One of the nice young men, Hector, set up their card table beforehand. He got out their chairs and laid everything out for them.

Hector always made sure they were alone in the far corner of the gym away from everyone else. A few other patrons were there playing ping pong or basketball, but nobody paid the ladies any attention. Others worked out in the fitness area. Saturday was a slow night, usually, for the community center. Nobody ever seemed to mind the card table setup in the gym.

The ladies waved at Hector as he walked by on his way back to the front desk. Priscilla checked out Hector's backside as he walked away. "Prissy, you scamp!" Levina said, pretending to slap Priscilla's hand.

"I ain't dead yet," she said.

The four of them roared with laughter. It was Nina's turn to deal, and she made quick work of it. Arthritis hadn't impacted her as badly as some of the others, so she usually got the lion's share of shuffling and dealing. She whistled "The Girl From Impanema" as she dealt the cards.

"Why do you always whistle that same song when we play, Nina?" Adele asked.

"I like it, I suppose," Nina replied.

Levina picked up her cards and carefully examined them. "I bid two," she proclaimed.

"You always say two. One of these days I am going to call you on it just to see if you can make the bid," Adele complained.

Nina laughed, "Even Hector could make two. Come on now, ladies, are we playing or flapping our gums?"

"Three," Priscilla said.

"Anyone beat that?" Nina asked.

The ladies all shook their heads. Priscilla laid down a two of hearts. "There's two for low," she said.

"Someone remember she got that. She won't win the trick, and we have to remember she got that one for her bid," Levina said.

"I'll remember," Nina assured.

The card game progressed, like it always did, for a few hours until they were almost ready to close the community center for the night. On this occasion, though, the women were in a strange mood. Their discussions ran to more macabre subjects.

Levina said, "What do you guys think of ghosts?"

Adele replied, "I think you don't have a ghost of a chance when you play against me in cards."

"I think they could be real," Priscilla commented.

Levina asked, "What do you think, Nina?"

"Well, I don't know about ghosts, but I have seen some strange things in my eighty some years on the planet, ladies. Strange things," Nina replied.

"Like what?" Adele asked, always one for a story.

Nina said, "When I was a young woman, I made ends meet as a typist. Sometimes, I would do some extra office work. Mostly, I would transcribe hand written documents into typed pages. I got paid a penny a page, and it was good wages back then.

"I wasn't choosy about when I worked. Sometimes, I worked on the weekends. Holidays, too. I even worked at night.

"I had my own portable typewriter, so I wasn't dependent upon my client's office materials. This was also a draw for some of the smaller outfits. One time, I got to transcribe pages for an author's novel.

"His name was Reuben Ignowski. Reuben wrote crime dramas, and had a recurring detective character that tied his books together. The Klondike Capers.

"Klondike was patterned after Ignowski himself, only 'sturdier'. I remember reading some of his pages and laughing at the contrast to his physical appearance, but seeing the author's ego shine through. Ignowski trusted me with the only copy of his handwritten novel, and I took the manuscript home with me.

"I read late into the night, typing as I went. This was not always the best idea as the stories contained murder and crimes, of course. Usually, a young lady found herself on the wrong end of a knife or gun or something more strange and unusual.

"Bizarre murders were Klondike's specialty. The pages I was typing that weekend night were about a girl who was found dead in an elevator, seemingly drown. I went to bed with that awful image in my brain. I woke up the next morning, ready to make myself a light breakfast and finish off a few more pages.

"I fetched the newspaper from the stoop and had my coffee and bagel while perusing the headlines. One jumped out at me immediately - 'Girl Found Drown in Elevator, Police Stumped'."

Levina said, "Ohh, goodness."

Nina continued, "Yes, strange coincidence. Or so I thought. I shrugged it off and got back to work. The detective in the story figured out that the hat check girl from the swanky restaurant across the street had been drowned in the huge fish tank in the lobby after hours. She had been taken in a cab and walked up to the office building, dumped in the elevator, and the killer thought he had gotten away scot-free.

"The details of the case burrowed in my subconscious, and I found I could not work very diligently that day. I decided to go out and see where the real murder took place. I wanted to check for other similarities.

"I took a cab to the office building and actually rode in the elevator where the girl was found. I didn't find anything, but really I had no idea what I was trying to find. Then, at the top of the office building, I got out and walked over to the picture windows and looked out at the city.

"I saw an upscale nightclub on the main strip and figured I had better check it out. I took the elevator down and walked across the street to the club. It was still early and they were not yet open, but I was able to walk in nonetheless. Employees were milling about, prepping for the night. There, in the middle of the club, was an enormous fish tank. And, they were filling it up.

"The maître d' noticed me and asked if he could help. I asked what happened to the fish tank, and he explained that they must have had a little leak so they were replenishing it. He said I should not worry as it would be ready for the evening's festivities and would not halt the opening of the club that evening. I thanked him and made my way to the police station.

"If you want to see what it feels like for people to treat you like an insane person, try explaining to the cops how you suspect the murder victim worked as a hat check girl and was drowned in the club's fish tank without being able to explain how you came across that knowledge. Still, I made a case and Detective Coughlin, the investigator assigned to the murder, assured me he would follow that lead - no matter how strange it seemed.

"I thanked him and went back to work. Or at least tried to. I wound up reading, mostly. Scanning the pages for other clues or something that would make sense of it all. I came to another murder scene.

"This was a hit and run incident that was seemingly unrelated to the hat check girl. In the novel, though, Klondike figured out that the man run down in the street was having an affair with the girl. This cast suspicion on the man's wife, who was a big socialite about town.

"I put down the manuscript and picked up the paper. I checked through it, and sure enough, there was an unsolved hit and run from the preceding night. A man who's grieving widow was a well-known socialite.

"I began to suspect that it was Reuben Ignowski himself committing the murders, then using it for material for his novel. How else could he be writing in such detail on unsolved cases? But what could I do about it?

"I decided it would be best for the police to sort it all out when the front door bell rang. I went to answer and was startled to see Reuben Ignowski there. I was shell shocked for a moment until he explained that he was there for the pages.

"I apologized for not having the work completed, but gave him what I had done already - eager for him to leave. I promised to have the rest done before the weekend was over and he left. I took a deep breath and called the police.

"Detective Coughlin I had spoken with earlier was surprised to hear me so soon. He was actually going to call me, he said. It did appear that the girl was a hat check girl at the club and the fish tank was looking to be the most likely place of her murder. He wanted to know if I had any further information.

"I told him about the hit and run incident and that they were connected. This time, he didn't probe for answers but instead just wrote down the details. He asked if I had anything else for him.

"It wasn't until then that I got the brilliant idea to read ahead in Ignowski's story to see how that murder investigation turned out. I asked the detective to be patient while I checked on something. I fetched the manuscript and read ahead a bit, scanning for details on the murders.

"The handwritten pages were difficult to read through quickly, but I made it to a point where Klondike was interrogating suspects. I glanced through and saw that the bassist for the jazz band was the culprit. That was enough for me and I went back to the phone.

"Detective Coughlin had been patient and waited for me. I suggested he investigate the bassist for a connection to the hit and run driver and the hat check girl and left it at that. He thanked me and hung up. I felt better than I had through the entire incident. I felt like I had made a difference.

"I also felt pretty good that the murderer hadn't turned out to be Reuben. My head spun on how he knew these things, but I knew I had to finish my work to be done with him. So, I set down and typed as quickly as I could.

"I went through the incidents which had already occurred in real life, this time gleaning details and motives. Klondike wrapped up that case and was about to solve another congruent mystery in the story. I prepared to read and type uncharted territory.

"In that portion of the story, a struggling author was making his living by writing crime novels similar to the cases Klondike was solving. The author hired a typist, who noticed the murders were identical with actual cases Klondike worked. So, she called Klondike and let him know about the author's inside info."

Levina interrupted, "No. Really?"

Nina said, "Honest. I grew pale, but kept typing. It didn't get terrifying until later. In the story, the typist was working feverishly to catch up after taking a hiatus to help the detective. I worked intensely to see what would happen.

"The typist was alone in her house when the author decided she was too much of a liability. His muse had been reality, and somehow the author just knew when something was going to happen. If that was revealed to the police, his livelihood would vanish. So, the author decided to kill the typist to silence her.

"I was alarmed, to say the least. I checked the door and windows, making sure the place was secure. I went back to typing the manuscript, eager to see what would happen.

"In the story, the typist was clicking away when the author cut the phone line. She was oblivious to this, but Klondike was starting to piece things together and was trying to call her. He noticed the line was dead and set out to investigate in person.

"I looked at my phone and wondered. I decided I was being silly and continued typing. The author jimmied the bedroom window and crawled in, unbeknownst to the typist. I stopped typing and listened. It was quiet. I was being ridiculous, I convinced myself. So, I continued transcribing.

"The author pulled out a straight edge razor, slowly advancing to the kitchen where the typist had made her office at the table. I was working at the kitchen table, and my heart skipped a beat. I imagined that Reuben was in the bedroom with a straight razor.

"My heart pounded in my chest now, not really understanding what was happening but suspecting I was in mortal danger. I had to know for sure. So, I stood up carefully and walked to the phone.

"I picked it up and placed it to my ear. My worst fears were realized when the line was dead. I gasped.

"I decided to run from the house, so I ran to the front and unlocked the door. I was stopped by Reuben Ignowski, straight razor unfolded and held high. 'I tricked you into thinking the killer was in the bedroom. It got you to unlock the door and let me in,' he said.

"I screamed and ran. Reuben slashed at me, narrowly missing me several times. I threw the pages of his manuscript at him hoping to slow him down, but he just laughed. I made it to the bathroom and locked the door. It was one of those easy to pick inside locks, but it still afforded me some time.

"Reuben found a coat hanger and untwisted the metal. He stuck the end into the lock and opened the door. I had back up so far as to actually be in the bathtub. He approached with the razor and I felt like my time had come.

"He raised the blade and I prepared to be killed when a shot rang out. Detective Coughlin had arrived just in time, shooting Reuben before he could murder me. Reuben crumpled to the floor, saying, 'Why does it always happen like this?'

"Detective Coughlin made sure I was okay, then left - just as confused as I was about what had transpired. Even though I no longer had a client, I had to finish typing the manuscript. After reordering the pages and figuring out where I left off, I did just that. The novel ended with Klondike shooting the author before he could cut the typist to ribbons.

The last page was the book dedication. It read 'To Nina: Thank you for being my muse and letting my stories come alive.'"

Adele said, "That was a fantastic story, Nina. Is it true?"

Nina replied, "Every word of it. I even dated Detective Coughlin for a while there afterward. I could have married him, except..."

"Except what?" Priscilla questioned.

"Except he never asked me," Nina said.

They all laughed again.

"I believe in ghosts," Levina said after a while.

"What makes you so sure?" Adele asked.

Levina replied, "Because of what happened to me. It was when I was a little girl, I used to visit my cousin in the summers while my mother and father tried to work extra hours during the harvest season. My aunt and uncle lived in a border town on the Arizona side called

Aborlito. I used to love to visit my cousin Fabiola who was just a year older than I.

"One summer, I went to stay for a while and hadn't packed enough clothes. I remember thinking I could buy some stuff when I got there because I had saved up some money babysitting. Aborlito had a sister town on the Mexican side called Aborlita.

"Fabiola and I planned a shopping expedition for that Friday night, when the tianguis would be open and thriving," Levina said.

"What are the tea an geese, Levina?" Priscilla asked.

Levina replied, "Tianguis. Oh, it is like a bazaar. A huge open market where many vendors come together. You can buy food, jewelry, clothing, all kinds of stuff. Mexico is filled with them, mostly in the bigger cities. They did exceptionally well in Aborlita, though, because it brought in shoppers from the U.S. side.

"The prices are good for locals, not such for tourists. Anyway, since Fabiola and I spoke Spanish, we were hoping I could pass for a local girl. I didn't have much money, anyway, so I thought that might help with my bartering skills. I couldn't pay if I really didn't have enough money, right?

"Long before Friday night came, Fabiola got in a fight with my aunt. It was over chores or homework or something, I don't remember. It was a teenage girl stubborn argument thing is all I recall. Anyway, Fabiola had to be right. As a consequence, she lost the opportunity to go to the tianguis with me on Friday. If she didn't straighten up, my aunt had told her, she would lose the opportunity to go out Saturday, as well.

"I was heartbroken. I didn't know what to do, and I had never been to the market place by myself. My aunt said she would go if she could, but she worked as a waitress on the weekends. My uncle said he would not go, either, but refused to give me a reason.

"At first, I thought I would stay with Fabiola. My aunt, however, said, she was being punished and it would not work if I were entertaining her. She gave me directions and even a little extra money to spend as encouragement.

"Friday night finally came, and I was nervous. Fabiola was a little mad at me, but really mostly upset with herself at that point. She waved goodbye to me, and my uncle told me to be careful. Then, I was on my way.

"I crossed the border without incident. In those days, you could walk in huge crowds across and I followed alongside a family for a bit to try and blend in. The throngs of people were anxious to see the sites and get some good deals. Street vendors were already set up on the outskirts, but people paid them little mind. They were ready for the big mercado. The tianguis.

"I was so nervous that I had to use the restroom. None of the permanent stores were open on Friday night. I saw some saloons that might have bathrooms, but I had sense enough to avoid those. I thought if I could find a restaurant, that might work. So, I set down along a street that looked promising.

"After successfully finding a suitable place, I came out and realized I was turned around on the street. I didn't know which way to go, and I no longer had the benefit of the crowd to follow. I began to get worried.

"That was when I first noticed the boy across the road. A street urchin, from the looks of him. He just stared at me and watched as I walked aimlessly through the sidewalks.

"The boy was about my age, maybe a little younger. Certainly, he was not threatening physically. Something about him made me shudder, though. I pretended to get my bearings and walked with conviction in a random direction so as not to let him know I was lost.

"I walked down the street, hoping to catch up with the crowd at some point and salvage the evening. At the very least, I hoped to find my way back to the border so I could make it home that evening. I was beginning to worry that I was going to be hopelessly lost in a strange town at night.

"The boy was following me, too, I noticed. Not overtly, but I kept catching glimpses of him in archways or on street corners. It was as if he just kept appearing places.

"I began to jog, hoping to find someplace faster. In reality, my heart was beating quickly and I was on the verge of panic. I think I might have run outright except I finally saw the tianguis.

"Relieved, I made my way to the marketplace. It was bustling with activity. There were wares of all kinds, and I mostly 'window shopped' through the open aisles.

"The boy had stopped across the street again and merely watched me as I went in. I tried to ignore him, but vowed to lose him in the crowds before the night was through. I didn't like the way he looked at me.

"At the end of one aisle, a young girl about my same size was selling a wonderful dress. She said it was hers, but she no longer needed it and wanted to know if a beautiful girl like me could use it. It was so pretty. We bartered a little, and she threw in a silver necklace with a cross if I purchased the dress and necklace as a set. I was thrilled at the good deal and thanked her. It didn't even cost all my money.

"The girl looked back behind me and noticed the boy. She shivered. 'Pobrecito,' she said.

"I asked what she meant and she shook her head and said no more. I looked back, and the boy was gone. I decided to take that as my cue to go home. I asked one of the adults selling pretzels from a long stick which way to the border. He told me, and it turned out to be a fairly straight shot home.

"Fabiola loved my dress and cross. I modeled them for her as soon as I got back. They fit perfectly and really complimented my complexion with their vibrant colors. My aunt was also thrilled at my success. My uncle could not have cared less.

"I didn't mention the boy. I worried that they may not believe me. Truth was, I began to doubt if he was real.

"The next day was Saturday, and Fabiola was exceedingly nice to her mother. We even washed and dried the dishes without being asked, I recall. It worked, and Fabiola was able to go out with me. Anyway, that night, we decided to go back to the tianguis. Fabiola wanted to see if she could find a dress like mine so we could pretend to be twins. I wore my new outfit so she could try and match it in the marketplace.

"Fabby and I went through the border, also without incident. Although this was her town, she let me lead as I was filled with pride from my successful trip the night before. She was very generous to let me be the expert.

"When it came to the point where I had crossed through another street to use the restroom in a restaurant, Fabiola questioned my judgment. I told her that it was a shortcut and I had tried it the night before. She relented and we went on our way.

"To reassure her, I told her what stores would be coming up around each bend so she knew I was aware of where I was. I kept checking for the boy, too, but I never mentioned this aloud.

"Fabiola kept telling me we were headed in the wrong direction, but I assured her it was just up ahead. Finally, we got to the intersection where the tianguis had been. It was gone.

"Fabiola and I walked up to the grounds and I got a chill. It was not just a regular park, you see. It was a cemetery.

"I went through the aisles, which were rows of tombstones now, trying to piece together what I had done the night before. I arrived at the end of the aisle and there was the boy.

"I was about to scream when Fabiola called out to the child. He turned and his face went white when he saw me. We walked up to him and I could see that he was real. He even smelled like a street child.

"He said, 'you gave me a start, senorita. I thought you were my sister for a moment. You see, she was buried in that dress and cross.'

"'Levina bought those last night,' Fabiola contested.

"'Sí, muchas gracias. That must be why I found this money on her grave. Now, I can eat for a few meals,' he said.

"'Pobrecito,' Fabiola said.

"I shivered. We never did make it to the real tianguis that trip. Just the ghost bazaar. I still have the dress, packed away somewhere. And I wear the necklace to this day," Levina said, holding the cross out for the others to see.

"Wow," Adele said.

"Those must have been some 'killer deals' all right," Priscilla said.

Nobody laughed this time.

After a moment, Hector walked over and started putting away some of the sports equipment. It was getting late and most everyone else had left. Hector would never come out and say they should leave, but the evening was getting late for sure.

Levina asked, "Adele, you ever have anything weird like that happen to you?"

Adele looked uncomfortable. "What is it?" Nina asked.

Adele replied, "It's just that, well, it is a little too personal."

"Too personal? We're old friends, Addy," Levina said.

Nina said, "No, I understand. If it is something you don't feel comfortable sharing with us, please don't. We don't want to make you upset, Adele."

Adele squirmed a bit in her seat. Finally, she said, "No, it's not that. Y'all are my family. It is just that it is still 'fresh' in my mind, you know."

"Understood." Priscilla replied.

Adele said, "No, its okay. It might be good for me to talk about. Especially with friends in a safe environment."

"What happened, Adele?" Nina asked.

"Look, if Adele doesn't want to talk about it, we should not make her," Priscilla objected.

"No," Adele replied, "Really, it is okay. I don't mind. This was a little after Seymour died. In fact, this is *about* Seymour after he passed away.

"Seymour was a good man, by and large, but I am sure you all know he had his faults. For one, he was never really there emotionally for me. He was a good provider and all, but I could not count on him to talk to, like I do with you all.

"This was never a problem until he retired. Then, we were faced with the fact that we had oodles of time to fill with each other and nothing to talk about. Seymour didn't even have any hobbies, so most of the time he didn't know what to do with himself.

"I still had you guys, our weekly pitch games especially, and my volunteer work. I had carved out a routine over decades and it was largely independent of Seymour. We both had some adjusting to do.

"I tried to get Seymour involved in church or with other men here at the community center. He would have none of it. He kind of retreated into himself and I was partly to blame. I should have been there for him."

"Oh, Adele, don't be so hard on yourself," Nina said.

Adele nodded. "I know you're right. We were both at fault. I can accept that now, but the time to fix it would have been decades before Seymour retired. At that point, our habits and our relationship were already etched in stone.

"Seymour was already dead before the incident. I just didn't know it. And, I really didn't know it wasn't an accident until after he died."

"What? I thought Seymour had some kind of heart condition and died in a car crash because of it, Adele," Nina asked.

"That was what the investigation turned out. But, truth be known, Seymour intentionally ran off the cliff in his car," Adele said.

"How do you know that, Addy?" Levina said.

"Seymour told me."

The ladies were silent, but the statement begged for more information. Finally, Adele took a deep breath and continued. She said,

"I was sitting in my sewing room, working on a project. And I looked up and there he was, standing in the doorway like he always used to do when he wanted me to stop and make him food or something. He said, 'I am sorry, Adele. I am so sorry to put you through this. I hope you can forgive me.'

"I was so stunned; I just stood and stared at him with my mouth gaping open. I got up to touch him, make sure he was real, and he just sort of wasn't there anymore. He wasn't anywhere in the house, either.

"I figured it was just some grieving widow thing. Something my mind was doing to try and cope. But, a couple days later, there he was again.

"This time, I was going to take a shower. He was sitting in the bath, naked as a jaybird. He looked at me with such sorrow in his eyes. He said, 'Adele, please forgive me. I should never have ended things this way. You don't deserve this. You don't deserve anything I have done to you.'

"Again, I was so shocked I was speechless. I closed my eyes and when I opened them, he wasn't there anymore. I forgot about the shower, and I went to bed.

"At that point, it was just a waiting game until I thought I would see him again. I kept checking rooms and seeing things out of the corner of my eyes. But Seymour didn't come back...for a while, anyway.

"About that time, I had convinced myself once again it was a coping mechanism, Seymour returned. This time, it was out in the garden. I thought I was safe out there. But when I looked up, he was sitting on the garden bench.

"Seymour said, 'Adele, please forgive me. I know I messed things up in our lives and I took the easy way out. I can't rest until I know that you can forgive me.'

"I said, 'I forgive you, Seymour.'

"That was all it took. He smiled at me and nodded. I hadn't seen him that pleased and happy in many, many years. I couldn't help but smile, myself. I got up and sat next to him on the bench. Neither one of us talked, but we both sort of figured things out then. A lot of things.

"You can't make up for mistakes or lost time, ladies. But sometimes, you can move on. You can forgive," Adele finished.

Priscilla started crying. "Oh, you. I can't believe you got me. I used to be made of stronger bilk. I just wish I had a story to tell you all, if nothing else than to switch from the sentimental stuff."

Levina got up and went to hug Adele. Nina smiled, nodding in approval.

Levina said, "We've all been touched by something special. I just wish there was some kind of proof. What we need is a pact."

Nina asked, "What kind of pact?"

"A death pact. Something where if one of us dies, we come back and let the others know for sure. Some kind of proof for the afterlife," Levina said.

"I can agree to that," Adele said.

"Me too," Priscilla nodded.

"It's agreed then. To the 'Death Pact'. When one of us, or all of us, go - we will come back here and let the others know about it," Levina said.

They all raised glasses and toasted to their new agreement. They went back to playing cards. "I bid three," Priscilla said.

"I can make four," Nina boasted.

"What is trump?" Adele asked.

Nina threw down an ace of spades.

Hector looked over at the empty card table and chairs. Every Saturday night, he was told to set it up. It remained empty until he closed up shop and then took it down. Some rich old lady had paid the community center a ton of money in her will to carry out these instructions. So, Hector obliged as part of his job. It seemed silly to him, though.

When it was closing time, Hector folded up the four chairs and collapsed the legs on the card table. He whistled "The Girl From Impanema" as he worked. Hector put everything away until next Saturday night, when he would repeat the seemingly meaningless chore. He paused for a moment as he thought he heard faint, distant laughter of older women. He shrugged and turned out the lights.

## YELLOW CAR

*October Fifteenth*

Timmy loved toy cars. His first word was "car". His world expanded when he discovered trucks. Race cars were his favorite.

Timmy played with a yellow sports car, making sounds of pure joy. What made his new favorite toy so special was that it looked just like Daddy's car. Timmy often said it was Daddy's race car.

Since Daddy moved away, the visits where he came were special. He rarely hit Timmy anymore. Plus, Mommy and Daddy didn't yell as much as they used to do. But sometimes Daddy still hit Mommy.

Timmy didn't like that.

Richard drove his yellow Lamborghini to his ex's house. If she knew what was good for her, she wouldn't raise a stink. She sure wouldn't want to cut off those sweet alimony payments. He grew angry just thinking about how much a dent it was putting into his lifestyle. How dare she? How dare they? Just how much did she think it took to raise a kid, anyway?

Suddenly, the wheel jerked out of his hand. Richard veered into oncoming traffic. He screamed, yanking the wheel with all his might as he barely avoided a semi.

Timmy was getting cranky. He thought of how Daddy had yelled at him last time. He took the car and swerved it across the carpet chaotically.

Richard fought to regain control of the Lamborghini. It seemed to have a mind of its own. It even seemed to lift off the pavement momentarily a couple times, coming down with a shower of sparks against asphalt protesting from the onslaught of metal.

Timmy was mad now. He took the yellow sports car and threw it. It flew across the living room floor and down the stairs to the front door, its small metallic body clanking as it bounced down the hardwood floor.

Mommy came running, seeing the entire scene. "What is wrong?" She asked.

The Lamborghini came to rest after tumbling end over end down the embankment. Richard couldn't understand it. The car seemed to literally fly through the air. He was so bewildered by it, he didn't even realize he was dying.

Mommy smiled. "No crying, baby. Everything is going to be fine now."

## THE CURSED AUDIO CASSETTE

*October Sixteenth*

Nowadays, not many have heard of the heavy metal band "Bolt". In the '80s, they were the quintessential hair band. With hits like

"Drama Queen" and "Stitch in Time", they rode the wave of success with style and a lot of hair spray.

The band had hits simultaneously on the top 40 and in the top five of the heavy metal charts. They participated in benefit concerts and even played for a couple variety shows. Many a kid could be seen imitating the signature move of Ivan Koller, the lead singer, as they crossed their forearms in an "X".

The band is no longer. The peak of their notoriety, however, was not a chart-topper. It was an audio cassette recording that was released, and subsequently recalled, entitled "Discharged Live".

During their performance of "Kiss the Frog", a young girl was crushed to death as fans pushed forward towards the stage. The sound of her screaming was inadvertently recorded on the track. It was used as evidence in the subsequent wrongful death suit against the band.

The record company called for the return of the live album from the stores. They also incented customers to exchange the audio cassettes for double their money back or equivalent amount in merchandise. Many took them up on their offer. The record company lost millions on the deal.

That wasn't the worst of it. Nobody knew exactly how despondent Ivan was after the incident. During their next performance of "Kiss the Frog", Ivan committed suicide on stage. He released a heavy light rig, crushing him.

In a strange twist of fate, the singer that replaced Ivan was also killed. Boris Gruber was hit by their own tour bus in a manner which defies explanation to this day. Following that, Bolt went through several lead singers though none seemed to "click" with audiences.

The legend of the audio cassette continued. There were several instances of suicide after people listened to the song. In many cases, the victims were otherwise happy, normal people.

The original recordings and returned audio cassettes have been destroyed. It is estimated that about two hundred remain in existence. If you find one, don't give it a listen.

# THINGS OF SAND AND SWEAT

## *October Seventeenth*

The desert was as flat as the listless sea. Heat waves rising off the asphalt were the only contrast in an otherwise featureless horizon. The road was a straight line disappearing into the distance.

Kealty really opened up the Indian. The motorcycle could do over 180, but even on this sparse and empty stretch of road Kealty couldn't bring himself to test it that far. As it was, he was pushing his own endurance.

The illusion of water on the road kept his focus. Kealty knew the mirage was a trick of the heat and asphalt. It was enough to keep his mind from lulling into unconsciousness.

How long had it been since he had slept? 48 hours? 72? He wasn't sure. He rode through the night and throughout the long day, stopping only briefly to eat, refuel, or for other necessities. So far, sleep had not been on that list.

The monster hadn't caught up with him. Not yet. He knew that it travelled faster than the limits of his motorcycle, though. When the creature arrived, it would be swift. Kealty had to be quicker.

He noticed small lumps dotting the highway for miles ahead. He had to lower his acceleration down to 80. Then, it made sense. They were dead groundhogs. Thousands of them. Roadkill.

He slowed to 60 just to permit weaving in and around the carcasses. He feared the newer bodies might be slick with blood and entrails, causing him to careen out of control.

The sun dipped below the horizon. Twilight would soon follow. Kealty felt the sting of sweat in his eyes, which had eroded through dust on his forehead behind the black bandana. Kealty pulled the bike over to the gravel shoulder.

He rubbed his eyes with the back of a leather glove. He tested his vision by looking around. He saw the carnage. Small bodies everywhere, ripe with blood and gore.

Then, the past finally caught up with him. He remembered a similar scene that he had witnessed several days before. He recalled blood. Bodies.

His vision had cleared with the things of sand and sweat. He could no longer outrun the truth. *He* was the monster.

# DRIP DRIP

## *October Eighteenth*

The summer night was tainted with the sweet smell of honeysuckle and the melodic chorus of crickets. Dogs barked lazily in the distance, keeping cats, raccoons or some other unseen nocturnal marauders at bay. It was not yet late enough for the occasional cacophony of giggling children to cease, though the sound was dwindling. A waft of grilled hamburgers rode on the wind, competing with the floral fragrance for dominance. The evening was afoul with the tapestry of rural Americana, but the night was no less malevolent for its amiable façade. The night harbored unspeakable evil. Evil so profound it oozed out from its very source, spilling to the ground.

Drip drip.

Daniel Cass read aloud from the journal he and his friend, Chris Hehn, had recovered from a secret recess in the cornerstone of the old general store on Main Street. It was also rumored that the place doubled as an apothecary at the turn of the last century. Flooding and water damage had left the old building unstable.

Even though it was an historic building, it was declared unsafe and slated for destruction. Chris was heartbroken, for so dearly he loved the town in which he was raised. Chris adored its people and their way of life. Daniel agreed with Chris, but did not share in his same infatuation with the place. It was hard for Chris to tear down the building, but that was his job. Daniel and Chris were in construction and demolition was a necessary part of that profession.

The two-man crew had unearthed the ledger in a sealed column underneath the cornerstone while demolishing the building with a small tractor and sledgehammers. Within the pages, they discovered that it was actually a journal by a man named Yotum Mueller with the last entry dating back one hundred years ago.

The discovery, however, would have to wait until their supervisor returned from the capitol city where he was visiting his sister. In the meantime, Daniel took the find home with him over the weekend.

Daniel related the journals contents to the eager ears of Chris and his wife Sarah, Daniel's wife Lila, and her brother Steve. The five of them sat in the near darkness under the canopy over the back porch, lit only by the Tiki torches Daniel had purchased at the hardware store for their weekly barbeque.

They were mostly hidden from each other in the gloom, except for the bright flowers of Lila's sundress and the sky-blue color of Chris' fleece vest. It was eighty degrees outside, even at night, yet Chris still insisted on wearing that stupid blue vest. He was a victim of his own fashion sense, Daniel thought.

Having already consumed a wonderful grilled meal, the group was content to sit and digest quietly as they listened, occasionally slapping at the rogue mosquito or two. They regarded the fascinating history of Joshua's Pride. Daniel continued reading, tilting the ledger towards a flaming torch to receive its full illumination. He mentioned the date of the entry, then read aloud.

> *Joshua's Pride was plagued by evil. The town was awash in widespread sin, which manifested itself in myriad atrocities. Dark deeds consumed the town, sucking its very soul dry as the desert sand on which it was founded. The ancestors of the village were desperate to rid themselves of their own vile putrescence, much as they would severe a gangrenous arm or leg in the hope of saving the rest of the body. We had to earn our own salvation through efforts of questionable judgment.*
>
> *Joshua's Pride would be damned were it not for the unearthly knowledge of Detlef Mueller, my learned cousin. Detlef knew of the old ways of some of our mixed ancestry, which had immigrated to the United States and settled in Joshua's Pride a single generation before my birth.*
>
> *My heritage held scores of superstitious rituals, which addressed problems such as the kind that had cursed the town. The church frowned upon these methods, as they were considered tantamount to consorting with the devil. Still, desperate times called for unconventional efforts. Detlef held the dark ways.*
>
> *Some of these beliefs advised that the best way to fight evil was with its twin. Detlef had agreed with them and thought that it would, indeed, take evil to battle evil. And Detlef knew how. He knew of a black ceremony that would last for a century, ridding them of evil for that time before needing to be repeated.*
>
> *This evil was to take the countenance of man. It would spawn a burly creature, faceless, nameless. A monster devoid of passion,*

*mercy, and a soul. Once summoned, it would conquer all evil before ceasing its onslaught. The method was an assortment of the belief systems of our mixed heritage, which included Jewish, Welsh, Danish, and even Pagan rites. Detlef would summon evil in the form of a unique monster, a Dustaphf di Meinger, a most powerful and malevolent form of Sin-Eating Golem.*

*The monster was to save Joshua's Pride through the most extreme of measures. The Golem would quite literally feed upon the parasite that plagued our humble village. It would destroy all evil, including those who concealed the seed of evil in their hearts. The evil would be extinguished as nothing could stop the golem, save for another more powerfully summoned Dustaphf di Meinger.*

*Since all men had held that malevolent kernel within them since being cast out of the garden, a substitute had to be made. A ritual was required, which would pass the sin of the people into an inanimate object and could then be destroyed. Once the evil was destroyed, Joshua's Pride could exist in peace.*

*The surrogate sin housing came in the form of either bread or fruit, but nothing derived from flesh as this was too close to the body and would not do. The evil was purged from the sinner's body into the food much pouring water into a pitcher. The Golem would walk the streets of the town, destroying evil by eating the fruits and bread laid outside. If the monster did not find the sin-laden offering, it would then seek an original source. This meant devouring the unfortunate person who had neglected to flush out the evil from their soul or place a suitable offering on the stoop.*

*Detlef called the Mayor to his home and explained the process. The Mayor, in turn, was to convince the townsfolk to perform the purging ceremony. He explained what they needed to do and to lay their offerings out on the stoop of their houses. He emphasized that nothing made of flesh could house the sin, or the monster would not accept it.*

*While Detlef departed, the villagers began to purge their sin into the food offerings. Nearly everyone participated, and through this task the village was afforded the first night of peace for quite some time. The overall mood was hopeful. They waited.*

*Detlef finally crested the hill and prepared the site for his ritual. It had begun raining violently, and I prayed that the rain would wash away the unholy ceremony. Lightning flashed over the hillside, but these warnings were also ignored. Detlef continued his preparations.*

*Detlef forged the countenance of a man from mud and straw. He then took off his own yellow raincoat and covered the creature, furthering its human form. Detlef spoke with archaic words. The spell had not been read aloud for nearly a century, but his lips formed the evil sounds adeptly.*

*The muddy imitation of a man began to rise.*

*The golem faced Detlef, who had let out a cackle at his own sorcery. The cackle turned to a piercing scream, more violent than any thunder that night, as the golem attacked and began to suck the evil right from Detlef's flesh and bones.*

*Detlef had forgotten to purge his own enormous sins into a food offering. The pain was to be equivalent to that sin, and Detlef could be heard screaming for miles. I ran. I ran and, heaven help me, I prepared an offering for the beast. My soul is damned. My efforts earned a place beside the devil, despite trying to buy my way to heaven. I appeased the monster and now my soul is damned.*

Daniel closed the journal, grinning maliciously.

"That rocked!" exclaimed Steve.

"It was cool, wasn't it? Man that legend has got to become public knowledge. I wonder how much was based on truth," Daniel replied.

"You know, that's the kind of junk that brings in tourist dollars, guys," stated Lila, who was currently taking business courses at the community college.

"Always after the monetary angle, huh Li?" Sarah jabbed.

Lila, showing uncharacteristic restraint, had decided not to pursue the comment.

"That rocked," Steve repeated.

Chris cleared his throat loudly. "Something else is weird about that. I don't know if anyone else caught it. Something very interesting."

Chris paused to milk the attention.

"The date you read from, Danny, well that was exactly a hundred years ago."

The group gasped with the realization.

"No kidding, it was, wasn't it?" Lila exclaimed.

"Yes, it is. To the year," remarked Daniel, checking the journal to verify Chris' statement.

"And," continued Chris, "Danny said that the dew staff thingy, what did you call it?"

"A Dustaphf di Meinger."

"Right. That golem would only be satiated for a century. Then, it would rise up and need to feed again."

The group yielded reign of the conversation to the crickets for a moment. With the absence of a moon, the darkness of night was overwhelming as were the innumerable stars in the cloudless night. They contemplated the possibilities.

They broke the silence with a simultaneous cackling roar. "And the funniest thing," Lila guffawed, "is that we're the closest house from Camel Rock to the east. Well, except for the Thomersons' across the street. They are just a smidgeon more east than us."

Camel Rock was the hill at the edge of town. It was so named because of its resemblance to a prostrate camel with a single hump. Lila and Daniel lived in the house at the town's edge, and it was, indeed, one of the two houses closest to the hill.

"You think Camel Rock was the hill from the story?" Sarah asked.

"What else could it be? There are no other hills around here, except for the mountain range in the distance. Those are too far away to walk to. Makes you glad we live down the street, west a bit. Hopefully, the monster will be full before he reaches us," Chris said.

Steve said, "I don't live too far from here, though. Hey, Danny, you got any fruit or bread? I've kinda got the munchies," he joked.

Daniel laughed. "Might have, Steve, but I don't think we have enough to fit all your sin into."

Sarah said, "Hey, Danny? Does that book say anything else? Does it say how to do the food ritual or anything like that?"

Daniel scoffed, but opened the journal just the same. He turned to face the torchlight. The night steadily consumed the light, so he scooted closer to its source. He flipped through the pages.

"Actually, it does. It has a few ceremonies outlined in detail. One of them is the food purging ritual. We can remove warts with this one. Here's one for keeping your livestock from wandering into your neighbors' land. Hey, guys, we could even make our own golem. Fun for the whole family!"

"So, just for grins, how do you perform the food ritual?" Sarah redirected.

It was apparent that she was somewhat apprehensive about the likelihood of a relentless monster invading the town. Daniel indulged her and informed the group of the procedure.

"That stuff is publishable. I'm thinking we don't hand this over, but keep it and try and get it printed. Might be worth some money. Mind if I look it over tonight, Danny? I won't keep it," Chris asked.

"Don't give it to him, Dan. He's got landscaping to do," Sarah stated, playfully hitting Chris in the arm.

The two had just purchased a house, after having lived in an apartment their entire married life. Chris was doing the landscaping, which currently consisted of a big muddy hole in his backyard.

"Come on, Danny Boy! Don't let the missus tell you what to do!"

Daniel nodded, shrugging. He had wanted to read more of it, but handed it over. Chris was trustworthy. It wasn't like he was ever going to skip his own beloved town. Chris deposited the journal in the inside pocket of his fleece vest.

The topic of conversation began to slip from the journal and its contents. They talked about work, people they knew, and common interests, only occasionally drifting back to the golem.

Eventually, their evening drew to a close and it was time for the guests to depart. They all meandered out to the front lawn to say their good nights. Across the street, Daniel noticed the eerie blue glow emanating from a window in the Thomersons' house, indicating that they were spending their Friday night watching television. The Thomersons didn't get out much.

Then, barely perceptible in the gloom of night, Daniel noticed a vague shape walking towards them slowly from the middle of the road. Had it not been for the bright yellow raincoat, he might have missed the advancing form entirely.

"What is that?" Sarah asked.

The group huddled together instinctually.

"You jerk, Dan!" yelled Chris, "You snuck in and called one of your friends to try and scare us."

"I swear, Chris, this ain't one of my jokes."

The figure continued forward.

Lila gasped, "It can't be!"

Chris shook his head in disbelief. "No, no way that's real. We're just imagining this. Too much heebie jeebies."

And still the form slowly advanced.

"Chris, we've got to get out of here!" Sarah demanded.

Daniel said, "You guys are just jumping to conclusions. It's only some guy in a raincoat. He probably thinks we're all crazy with the way we're carrying on. It's just some guy."

Lila grabbed Daniel by the arm, spinning him towards her. "Dan, the guy is wearing a raincoat! A yellow raincoat! There's not a cloud in the sky!"

Daniel gazed skyward at the heavenly expanse of the universe, fully visible in the moonless, cloud-free evening sky.

The thing in the raincoat continued towards them.

They froze, dumbfounded and immobilized with fear. It still proceeded. While the form was still indiscernible, the raincoat was close enough to see the sheen of its wet surface.

Sarah fell to her knees, shaking uncontrollably. Chris managed to pull her back up, holding her protectively to his chest.

"Look, it's still only one guy. You two work construction and I'm no slouch myself. I say we can take him," Steve said.

It drew closer. The black mass underneath the hood of the raincoat had no eyes.

"I'm not convinced it's an inhuman monster, guys. Let's go talk to him. You'll see," said Daniel.

"Sure thing, Mr. Brave Guy. You and Steve go ahead. I think I'll stay back here with the ladies," Chris stated.

Lila grasped Daniel's arm again, firmly. "No, Danny! No!"

Lila had not needed to hold Daniel back, for he had not convinced himself that the form wasn't an inhuman monster, either.

Steve looked at Daniel and Chris. "Well, I'm not going out there without some backup," he said.

It was closer now, and they could see a seething mass of mud in the form of a man. Its raincoat was soaked. It seemed to be raining on the thing, yet no drops fell from the sky – only from the creature itself.

Drip drip.

Lila pointed at the thing and said, "That's not human, Dan!"

By this time, her statement was obvious. The golem was close enough so that they could hear its footfalls. The sound made a splattering moist noise on the asphalt leaving muddy footprints in its wake. Sarah screamed, wrenching away from Chris and shielding her face with her hands.

"Oh please, do something!" Lila shrieked.

The creature drudged forward, dripping. Its muddy hands resembled mittens in their vaguely human shape.

The monster changed its path, veering for the Thomersons. They let out a collective sigh. "It's just some guy that fell in the sewer. Just some guy that fell in the sewer," Daniel repeated.

Although in their hearts they all knew this to be untrue, the horror of reality helped convince themselves to believe it. The delusion didn't last long, unfortunately. The monster began beating at the house, leaving bold streaks of glop on the door as it pounded.

Mr. Thomerson flung open the door, a hunting rifle at the ready. Even from across the street, they saw his eyes widen. To his credit, he did manage to shoot a round off in the torso of the thing. It ineffectually burst through the back of the raincoat, however, as the monster seized Mr. Thomerson's arm.

The creature attacked Mr. Thomerson. Mud enveloped the man, who fell to the ground in a large syrupy puddle. Then, the oozing mass rose up and formed back into the golem. The yellow raincoat seemed to form out of nothing, and began to shimmer with moisture again, catching the sparse light sources around it. The monster pushed through the screen door and into the house.

"The Thomersons are first because they are more east. We're next, Dan! We're next!" Lila sobbed.

Sarah quit screaming and grabbed Chris, leading him running to their car. Within seconds, they were both in and speeding west towards their home and away from the horror. Daniel shook his head in amazement, having barely registered their departure.

Daniel, Lila, and Steve still stood on the porch, witnesses to the horror across the road. Mrs. Thomerson screamed from within the house across the street. Lila put her hands over her ears to block out the sound.

"We've got to get in the house, barricade it from that thing!" Steve commanded.

The three shook themselves out of their petrified fear into defensive action. They retreated to the house just as the monster emerged from the Thomerson's house. It began to walk slowly towards them.

The trio began piling objects against the front door; a coffee table, a baker's rack, vacuum cleaner. The makeshift barrier began to look insurmountable. They panted and gasped, awestruck with terror.

"Look, what if we did that ritual thing? We've got to purge our sins in some bread or fruit!" Lila demanded.

Steve nodded his head in agreement. Daniel tried to understand what was real. None of this made any sense.

A slam from outside at their front door startled them all. The violent crash repeated, followed by another. The thing was trying to break into their house.

Daniel's eyes broadened. "We – we don't really do anything bad. We're good people. It won't hurt us," he said.

"All of us have sinned!" Steve informed.

Lila shook Daniel, desperately trying to bring him back to reality. "This is happening, Danny! It's trying to break in now!"

The crashing continued. "But," said Daniel, "Chris and Sarah have the journal."

The banging on the door continued, they heard cracking and splintering of wood. It was going to get in.

"DANNY!" Lila screamed.

"Dude, you told us how to do it! Let's just remember and do it," Steve yelled.

Lila shrieked again, the front door partially gave way at the hinges. The creature pounded repeatedly at the obstacle. It could be seen now, through the broken entryway.

"Okay, okay!" Danny shouted. They ran to the kitchen in search of food.

"Grab any bread or fruit you can and follow me back to the foyer!" Daniel instructed.

Lila protested, "It's in the foyer, Danny!"

"We have to put the food in the entrance to the house or it won't work! HURRY!"

They frantically searched the pantry, refrigerator, and shelves for the necessary ingredients to purge their sins. Remarkably, the three then ran back to where the monster had almost gained entry.

Daniel laid his unfinished watermelon half, a leftover from this evening's cookout, on the ground. He saw Lila place some frozen packages of hot dog and hamburger buns she had produced from the freezer onto the floor. Steve dropped something on the ground, as well, to add to the offering.

The monster had broken through the door entirely, and cast it aside. The pile of flotsam was all that lay between them and the great beyond.

In the distance, beyond the violent crashing and breaking, they began to hear sirens wailing. Mrs. Thomerson must have called the cops before it got to her. "Repeat after me!" Daniel screamed.

Daniel spoke the incantation as best as he could remember. Steve and Lila repeated each phrase. The monster freed itself from the debris and advanced towards them.

Lila cried. Steve said, "What now, dude?"

"That's it! That should do it. Back up, it has to get to the food unimpeded!" Daniel said.

They drew back a few steps and watched the golem enter the house completely. It stopped at the pile of food, moving its hooded head towards the offering. It stood, motionless for a moment. The sirens drew closer.

The monster bent over, grabbing the watermelon first. In one gulp it devoured the fruit, shell and all. Daniel gasped as he actually felt a lightening sensation in his chest. Somehow, he knew that it had worked – at least for him. He let out a long sigh of relief.

The creature turned and stepped towards the frozen packages of buns. It hesitated, and then clumsily seized the bread. It devoured them, including the plastic wrappings, in a sloppy slurp. Daniel heard Lila gasp in surprise and reprieve.

The sirens came to a stop in the street in front of the house. Red and blue flashing lights danced on the ceilings, finding entrance through the windows. The monster sidestepped towards Steve's offering.

The golem hesitated once more, stooping only to retrieve the offering. Daniel saw what it was for the first time – a box of Twinkies. Car doors slammed outside.

Daniel felt a sinking feeling in his gut. He held his breath. The monster cast the treats aside and advanced towards Steve.

"Steve, Twinkies are made with animal fat! You can't use any flesh of an animal!" Daniel scolded.

Lila yelled, "Steve, why didn't you find something else?!"

Steve backed up in horror. The monster continued towards him. "I can't help it if you guys don't eat healthy!" he shrieked, running towards the kitchen.

"Get something else!" Lila demanded.

Daniel grabbed Lila and said, "He can't, Lila. It has to be at the entryway. It's too late."

"No!" she screamed.

Two police officers entered through the broken doorway, their pistols drawn.

Lila pointed at the creature poised to attack her brother in the dining room. They dutifully aimed their guns and one of them shouted, "Halt! Police officers. Turn around!"

It did not cease. Steve screamed in anticipation of the inevitable. The policeman ran towards the raincoat-clad creature, which then turned to greet them. They saw the muddy, faceless mass underneath the hood. One cop dropped his arms as well as his jaw in shock. The other aimed his weapon at the monster's chest, the coat having been already marred by a rifle shot.

The creature strode towards the policemen. The one policeman pulled the trigger, sending a bullet through the creature and into the wall next to Steve. He dove for cover. The second policeman turned to face Daniel, an expression on his face as if to ask "What is it?"

The creatures attack was as swift on the interlopers as it had been when it devoured the Thomersons. It seized both men simultaneously, coating them in a covering of mud and filth Their bodies seemed to melt into the floor. Then, the monster rose and took its usual form once again.

Lila hid her face in Daniel's chest, averting her eyes from the horror unfolding. The golem turned once again, returning to the task at hand.

"Steve, run!" Lila yelled.

Steve tried to oblige, but the monster halted his progress. Muck poured over Steve like caramel coating an apple. His form eroded into an indistinguishable pulp on the ground.

"No!" Lila roared.

She ran from Daniel, grabbing a fireplace poker from the living room and rushing towards the beast. Daniel flung himself around her, utilizing every ounce of strength he had to restrain his wife.

She grunted in anguish, struggling to save her dying brother. "It's too late!" Daniel hollered.

She continued to squirm. Daniel grabbed her face and slapped it. "It's too late! You can't interfere. The monster will kill anyone who interrupts its work. You can't do anything, Lila!" he said.

She looked at Daniel, the red and blue lights of the patrol car outside glistening along the lines of her tear-streaked cheekbones. She nodded her head, resigning to Daniel's statement.

"It took our offering." Daniel whispered.

Lila looked into his eyes. "But at what cost, Danny? Our souls? How can there be a suitable sacrifice for everything bad we've done in our lives? What have we earned through our efforts?"

The crickets sung in full chorus. A sweet honeysuckle aroma saturated the air. It was dark. So dark that it was difficult to see the creature headed west towards town. It would be almost invisible were it not for the bright yellow raincoat. Rivulets of glop ran down from vaguely hand-like shapes, seeping from saturated mud.

Drip drip.

# BOARD STIFFS

### *October Nineteenth*

Odin's Beard was only technically open until 9pm, but it was well past that now. The store, specializing in fantasy board games, had a large table in the back where the proprietors hosted gaming tournaments, card trading events, and open game nights where patrons could "try before you buy".

Dudley, Colton, and Lon were taking advantage of the store's hospitality. The bored clerk stayed glued to his iPhone, barely noticing the whimsical world unfolding in the back. The trio was deep into their Cthulhu Mythos playing the horror board game "Lair of Shadows".

The cold night was foggy, further distancing itself from reality. The three young men continued to roll the dice, taking turns moving pewter miniatures. They occasionally drew cards.

The trio, engrossed in their game, didn't hear the bell ringing as the glass front door of the shop opened. In walked a man in a heavy trench coat. He donned a wool trapper cap and sported a heavy black beard. He looked as if he could bend railroad ties without too much effort.

"Can I help you, sir?" the clerk asked, finally looking up from his smart phone.

"I wanted to test a game. Anyone playing?" he asked in a gruff voice.

The clerk motioned back. The big man nodded. Finally, Dudley, Colton, and Lon noticed him.

"May I play a few turns?" the large man asked.

The three players looked at each other. "He does resemble Salvatore in the game," Lon offered.

"Thanks," the large man said.

After a few turns, it became apparent that he had played many times before, as he was the strongest of the four. Dudley began to get frustrated. Colton tried to lighten the mood, but Dudley hated it when he broke character. Lon was indifferent, seeing as he was losing anyway.

Finally, the large man's luck ran out. His character was fatally cursed. With a sigh, he got up and thanked them. He turned to leave.

"It's a good thing you didn't win," said the clerk.

"Why's that?" the big man asked.

"The ghosts hate losing," replied the clerk.

The large man turned back. Three skeletons continued to play the board game. The big man fainted.

## WHERE DID YOU BURY ME?

*October Twentieth*

Goody Cole was imprisoned as a witch in Hampton, New Hampshire, in February of 1656. Her sorcery was said to have sunken ships, caused disasters, and led many to their deaths. She was not executed, but rather her properties were seized and sold to pay for incarceration. She died six years later, forsaken and abandoned. She was buried in a secret location. But this is not where her story ends.

For nearly three centuries, Goody was silent in her hidden interment. Something would happen that would awaken her slumber. Goody was posthumously pardoned for being a witch.

The road to Hell is paved with good intentions, some say. This was certainly the case with the removal of the title of witch from Goody Cole's name. She didn't want to be cleared of her witchcraft. She was proud of it.

Goody's spirit returned to the earth to restore her bad name. She had worked hard to wreak havoc and mischief. Taking the moniker of witch away from her was a slap in the face.

The witch's ghost came back to retrieve her corpse. Once reunited, she would transcend death to become a formidable sorceress. Then, she would exact revenge on Hampton. One thing lay between Goody and her revenge – she would have to find her grave.

In 1939, the sightings of a white haired, blue-eyed woman began. She was wandering the cemetery. Goody had come back.

Townsfolk say that they have seen the old woman walking through headstones and the wrought iron gates of cemeteries. They say she is searching frantically, scanning the graveyards in search of her hidden burial plot.

In 1963, a police officer responded to a complaint of an intruder at the cemetery. The policeman approached the trespasser, which turned out to be a very old woman. She turned to him, face pale and ghastly. She asked him, "Where did you bury me?"

The officer reported the incident and was ridiculed, despite the fact that his hair had turned pure white. Several others claim to have seen her roaming gravesites around Hampton. If you should run across her late one night in a graveyard around Hampton, just don't help her find her body.

# HOUSE WINE

### *October Twenty-First*

The table hosted seven, which was an odd number for a wedding party. Dane was not one for superstition, but he did prefer even numbers - especially for circumstances such as this. There should be more, but as both bride and groom had waited until later in life to find each other, many of the family had died off in the interim. Three out of four of their parents were gone, leaving all of the wedding responsibilities to fall upon Norbert Tennyson.

Norbert Tennyson never mentioned how his wife had passed; to be fair, Dane never asked. He had barely met the father of the bride. It was his best mate, Harrison, that was to marry into the Tennyson family fortune. It was his wedding which drew Dane out of his virtual hiding.

Not really hiding, per se, but more of a voluntary absence from society. Dane Lowell, who had unmasked the murderer of Mulberry Manor, but not in time to save the lady fair. Lady Hildegard Mulberry, ninth and final victim.

Dane had been unable to solve the mystery in time to spare her life and had therefore society considered himself a failure and more than just a little responsible. It was as if he had used the brodequin on her himself.

That botched case stained an otherwise untarnished career. Society had a short memory, and if Dane could simply wait out the worst of the headlines, he could return to the states and resume his life. He hoped, anyway. He knew he would never escape the nightmare of finding Lady Hildegard Mulberry just a little too late.

Rounding out the wedding table was Harrison's bride to be, Pamela. Her younger brother and sister, Argus and Felicia, were also in attendance. Pamela's school companion, Allison Bean, was present. Harrison had no brothers or sisters, so when his parents died he only had Dane, his good friend. So, the auspicious occasion was enough to pull the now infamous detective out of hiding.

"Dwight, bring the house wine. We need to celebrate! Tomorrow is the beginning of the twentieth century...and the marriage of my beautiful daughter to a fine, upstanding man." Norbert Tennyson announced.

Dwight, an elderly manservant, obliged bringing forth a few unseen bottles of something red. Dane was already thinking of a proper toast when he spotted the label. Vargas. From Argentina.

Despite his better judgment, Dane spoke up. "I must apologize, but I cannot drink this wine."

Shocked faces stared back at him from around the table. "Sir?" Dwight questioned, holding the label for closer inspection.

"This is from the vineyards of Pascal Vargas. I don't think anyone here should drink of it," Dane commented.

"But sir," Dwight protested, "it is the house wine."

"What's wrong, Dane. Is it poison?" Harrison asked.

Dane shook his head. He felt foolish already, but explaining the rationale behind his decision would paint him downright insane. Still, he could not risk the alternative. He could not drink the wine.

"Then it is not to your taste?" Norbert asked, incredulously.

Reluctantly, Dane nodded.

"Then, you sir, are a cad. You insult the family taste, this establishment, and my daughter on the eve of her wedding. I shall not stand for it," Norbert said standing and throwing his chair violently to the floor.

He withdrew a dueling pistol from his capacious coat and walked over to Dane, aiming it at his forehead. It was not the first time Dane had a loaded weapon pointed at him. Somehow, he knew, it would not be the last.

"Father, no!" screamed Pamela.

"Please, sir," Harrison begged.

Dane remained motionless, locking eyes with Norbert. He could see that the man had never taken a life. Never *could* take a life. Now, the challenge was, finding a way to salvage the night and let this poor fellow out of the situation with his dignity intact.

"Of course, I would never shoot a man in cold blood. A duel. You've disgraced us all and there must be blood atonement," Norbert said, somewhat less forcefully now.

Nobody spoke or moved. Norbert's hand began to tremble. Dane had to act before Norbert's nerves betrayed his true emotion or worse - yielding enough pull on the trigger to finish the job for good. The only thing Dane could think of was honesty. Blast!

"I can see you are a man of integrity. Tables be turned, I would do the same thing. Your daughter, after all. And I, a relative stranger, upsetting things without explanation," Dane began.

Norbert replied, "Quite."

"If you allow me to tell a tale detailing why I cannot palate Vargas wine, then you can do as you choose. If you still wish to duel, I will oblige. If you wish me to leave, I shall do so and never darken your doorstep again. Will that be satisfactory?" Dane explained.

Norbert stared. Finally, he nodded succinctly. "Thank you. You may return to your seat. I may be a cad, but I am a man of my word. I will not flee. My fate will be entirely yours upon the completion of the tale. A true story, though fantastic elements would suggest otherwise."

Norbert slowly picked up his chair and sat back down. He was trying to figure out what had just happened, but was relieved that he hadn't truly painted himself in a corner. Sweat ran from his brow. The poor man, Dane thought.

"As you may know, I am a detective by trade and not bound to borders for my clientele. I have had the benefit of solving some high profile cases, which allowed me to travel to solve similar mysteries abroad."

Harrison contributed, "You may have heard of them. The Hamblin Concert Affair and the Oxford murders when they began to allow female students on campus."

"Thank you, Harrison," Dane said, dismissively.

"And more, there was the time-" Harrison continued.

"Please," Dane interrupted, "allow me to finish."

"Sorry," Harrison replied.

"No worries. The details aren't important. Suffice it to say, that in the early days of my career, I was afforded the luxury of being able to pick and choose where I wanted to go and which cases I wanted to investigate.

"I had just wrapped up a case in Alaska during the gold rush, where jumpers had murdered a land owner then forged paperwork to stake their claim illegally. I was weary of the cold, so when I heard about a string of murders in Latin America, it piqued my interest. Someplace nice and warm, I thought.

"It was in the wine country of Santa Luna, Argentina, where I found myself headed. The strange events centered around a vineyard, run out of an old mission that had been abandoned after Argentina broke free from Spanish reign. Pascal Vargas himself hired me.

"The people of the village, many of whom were under the employ of Pascal, were falling prey to a killer in their midst. The case proved exceedingly difficult. Clues were scarce, and those I did manage to uncover seemed to contradict each other. All I knew for certain was that people were dying. And they were afraid.

"The fear was affecting vineyard productivity to the point where Pascal had to do something. Hiring me was just the start, and if I couldn't show results then he would seek another alternative. I knew the clock was ticking.

"Pascal had sent with me a beautiful senorita by the name of Marguerite. I had assumed she was his daughter, but later found out how mistaken I was. She shared the same last name through marriage, as did many other young women in the household. Vargas was a bigamist."

Allison let loose a cry of surprise. Dane smiled, and continued, "Marguerite was my guide and translator. She led me around town, assisting in various inquiries as I tried to establish patterns. In criminal investigation, patterns yield perpetrators."

"What did you find out, Dane?" Harrison asked.

Dane said, "That everyone in town thought they knew something, but nobody really did. Until, that is, I came across Peitro. He was an older gentleman who ran the town livery. He sought me out.

"Peitro would not speak with Marguerite around, so I dismissed her for the evening. I was lucky that the old man had a rudimentary command of the English language. I had picked up a few Spanish phrases myself, and together we were able to converse at a very basic level.

"Peitro led me down the path that would reveal the truth. He informed me that Pascal Vargas was not the saint that many painted him to be. I listened, for I had formed a similar conclusion on my own.

"He alluded to the fact that Pascal had acquired land through shady dealings. Peitro said that if anyone crossed Pascal, they would most likely wind up dead or missing entirely. Even Peitro's hermano was killed under mysterious circumstances.

"The most astonishing thing he told me, though, was that at least half of the vineyard was growing over an old campo de bastilla - a battleground. There were scores of unmarked dead buried in the fields from the Argentine Battle for Independence. Spanish and Argentines alike, laying beneath unmarked graves after falling in battle."

"Oh, how awful." Felicia said.

"Indeed," said Dane, "awful. Not the strangest part, as it would turn out. The most bizarre occurrence was the killer. Or should I say killers."

"Really?" Argus asked.

"Quite. Do you recall how I said that my clues seemed to contradict each other? That was under the supposition that there was only one murderer in Santa Luna. In fact, there were three," Dane said.

"Three killers?" Harrison asked.

"Yes, two for the current state of affairs and one more- but I get ahead of myself. Allow me to continue.

"I was displeased by what I was learning about Pascal Vargas, but I had given my word as to finding out the killer. I vowed to cut the investigation short by setting a trap. To catch the murderer in the act.

"I laid the bait - Marguerite herself, who waited seemingly alone in the village square after sundown. I hid in the shadows, ready to leap into action. Our efforts proved fruitful, and soon I apprehended a stout little man known as Romero Santos. He was jailed and I thought my job was complete.

"The next morning brought news of another murder, which must have occurred after capturing Santos. It was Peitro. He had been killed.

"Peitro's body was found in the vineyards themselves. My initial suspicion turned to Pascal himself, but I soon dismissed it. Pascal Vargas had not made a name for himself by being sloppy. If he wanted Peitro dead, Vargas could have made Peitro simply disappear.

"I returned to my original clues, reexamining them under the realization that there was more than a single murderer. The facts led me to Malvina Ortero. Malvina had already been questioned in a routine inquiry, so for me pressing another session in lieu of recent events didn't appear to worry her.

"Marguerite acted as translator while I tried to draw out answers on where she had been the preceding night. Malvina didn't intentionally evade questioning, but it quickly became apparent that there were gaps in her memory.

"Malvina offered Marguerite and I a glass of wine - the Vargas label. Marguerite shook her head and politely declined, but I was accepting of her hospitality. I held the glass, but didn't drink from it initially. Soon, however, I smelt its wonderful bouquet and succumbed to the sweet nectar.

"My head went blank after that. I awoke on the floor with Marguerite standing over me. A broken bottleneck was in her hand. The ringing pain in my temple drew the rest of the picture. She had bashed me over the head with the wine bottle.

"She raised the jagged edge as if to deliver a fatal stab when I pleaded with her to stop. She looked confused, at first, then relieved. I rolled my aching head to the side and saw Malvina. A knife jetted out between her ribs. She was dead.

"I slowly retreated from malaise and Marguerite could see that I was back to my normal self. She told a horrifying tale. Marguerite related how shortly after drinking the wine, both Malvina and I acted as if in a trance. We both tried to kill her. I remembered none of this, but glanced at my pocket watch. I had lost twenty minutes inexplicably.

"What if, I theorized, there was some supernatural component to the murders in Santa Luna. What if the unmarked dead in the soil of the vineyard were somehow permeating the grapes with their evil presence? What if anyone who drank from the wine became possessed and sought malice?

"It was a theory that I feared would bring me ridicule, but instead was met with understanding. Pascal Vargas admitted to having lost some time of his own and woke up confused. I suspected there was more to the story, but didn't press it.

"Vargas agreed to destroy the current stock and rotate his vineyard to the opposite field. He promised never to grow grapes over the unmarked dead again. I bandaged my aching head, collected my pay, and left accordingly."

"Well, if he promised you he wouldn't grow grapes over the battlefield, why do you still fear that label?" Norbert asked.

"Because I don't trust him, Mr. Tennyson. Unlike you and me, Vargas was not a man of his word," Dane said.

"Daddy, I don't want to commemorate this occasion with the Vargas wine," Pamela offered.

Several other guests murmured in agreement. Dane could see that Norbert was growing red with embarrassment. Dane had to diffuse the situation and still protect the host's integrity.

"I am sure, Mr. Tennyson that a man of your exquisite taste would have no problem picking out something else. Why don't you accompany Dwight to the wine cellar and give him some direction," Dane suggested.

"Right," Norbert said, and as he got up Dane was surprised to feel that Norbert actually patted him on the back on his way to the cellar.

Dane smiled. "Nicely done, old man," Harrison complimented.

"I believe you are my senior, sir," Dane retorted.

"What shall we do with these three bottles, then?" Felicia asked, looking at the Vargas vintage.

"Throw them into the fire," Pamela suggested.

Argus grabbed two bottles and Felicia seized the third. As if christening a ship, they counted down from five and flung the bottles into the flames. Smoke billowed out and took the shape of a skull. The plumy apparition growled audibly before dissipating back into the fire.

Argus and Felicia backed up instinctually. Pamela shuddered and Harrison put an arm around her for comfort. Dane wondered how many other public houses in London, or all across the country for that matter, had the Vargas label as their house wine.

# BREADCRUMBS

*October Twenty-Second*

Michalina tore another piece of the loaf that should have been her dinner. She dropped it. Its path meandered out of sight.

She didn't fear birds eating the crusts. It was already dark. As long as she made her way out before sunrise, she would be okay.

The October night was cool enough to see one's breath. The leaves had already fallen, which made the path easier to see by the light of the half-moon. The shadows of the leafless branches crisscrossed at her feet like a spider web.

Michalina tilted her head. She thought that she heard something. She stood motionless.

She decided that she would hum, having never mastered the skill of whistling, to occupy her mind. She spun a wordless tune that hung in the night air. She continued to spread breadcrumbs.

Another branch splintered. "I hope that's not you, Marchello. Or you, Papa."

Somehow, she knew it wasn't.

Michalina walked faster. More cracking through the woodlands as something pursued. She started to run.

It gave chase. In a clearing, Michalina fell to the ground. The stub of her bread loaf tumbled away.

She turned back. A large, red ogre came from the trees. It drooled when it saw her.

Her father had always taught Michalina to be brave. She didn't cry out. She didn't tremble.

The ogre was mostly bald, but patches of hair clumped about. It had lost an eye, probably the result of a territorial battle. It was clad in bearskin.

The ogre advanced, relishing the hunt. Michalina prepared herself. It came close.

From underfoot, a boy twirled through the monster's open legs in a figure eight. The ogre looked down, confused. The boy whistled.

The chain when taught, pulling the ogre down. From out of the shadows, a large hulk of a man came out holding the end of the chain. He wrapped it around a stump.

Then, he lifted his rather large axe and finished the job.

"That's quite a bounty we've collected for today," Marchello said.

"Yes, with that and the witches, our coffer's nearly full," replied Papa.

Michalina stood up. She placed loving arms around her family. It wasn't easy, but it was a living.

# LAIR OF THE MANDRAKE

### *October Twenty-Third*

Reece Hudson had been hired collectively by the parents of the Breckenridge ghetto. They couldn't afford his fees individually, but there were enough missing young men that they could pool their resources for his service. They didn't trust the police to resolve the matter.

The authorities dismissed the disappearance of several of the neighborhood youth as being gang related. The West Jackals had a presence and it was assumed these children were either victims of the gang or had enlisted themselves. Little effort was made to solve the case.

Reece's retainer was enough to cover expenses. The bonus fee in solving the disappearances would help him to relocate elsewhere. He was tired of the inner city.

His investigation led him to the old Crawford Bakery. Reece was told it was now a crack house. He went inside.

Even though the place was trashed with garbage, nobody was there. Reece continued forward. He walked to the back.

The kitchen had a cellar door. With considerable effort, he lifted it. He propped the door open with a plank that served as a shelf.

Wooden slats led down into darkness. Reece flicked on a flashlight and descended. Above him, the shelf board collapsed. The heavy door fell with a loud clatter.

Reece dropped his flashlight, which bounced down the stairs. It rested on the ground. It illuminated dust and cobwebs in a soft yellow cone.

Reece felt out cautiously in the dark. He found the ground, which was earthen. He dug at it absently with his foot.

Reece reached down and grabbed the light. The beam crossed over a woman. He gasped.

He directed the beam at her. He realized, it wasn't really a woman. It was just a trick of the light. Shadows made it look like a woman, but it was a large uprooted plant. The leaves and flowers resembled hair.

Reece directed the light across the floor. Several skeletons and desiccated bodies lay strewn about. In the dirt floor beside them, plants were going through bodies.

He found the young men's corpses. Reece Hudson had solved the case. Now, he thought, he just had to get out of this cellar.

The mandrake had other plans.

# ROBERT JOHNSON'S BARTER

*October Twenty-Fourth*

Rock and Roll as a music form owes its debt to the blues. The blues owes it debt to Robert Johnson. Robert Johnson owed his debt to the Devil. That debt was paid in full.

Robert Johnson had no musical talent to speak of, but he did have a passion for it. It was an appetite so consuming that it tore him apart to where he had to do something. He had to make a deal.

Some say a crow whispered the secret to him. Johnson was all ears. He stole a guitar, as the raven had instructed. And he went to a crossroads near Dockery Plantation in Mississippi at midnight to meet the Devil.

The Devil had a bargain. In exchange for his immortal soul, Johnson would be a famous musician. Inexplicably, he could somehow play the guitar, sing, and write songs. He would be immortalized.

But, there was a limitation to the gift. He could only use it until he was 27 and then the Devil would collect on the debt. Robert was a young man, though, and it seemed like a ways off.

The deal was struck. Johnson wrote a soft, melancholic tune known as "Cross Roads Blues" about the incident. It launched his success and forged the music style known as the blues which then gave birth to rock and roll.

Fame was not to last. Johnson enjoyed the life for a time, though. Perhaps too much. He invented the rock and roll lifestyle. But it caught up with him.

Johnson had a tryst with the wrong woman. Her boyfriend poisoned Johnson at a juke joint in a jealous rage. Johnson died at 27 years of age.

Since then, the blues and rock and roll have given rise to many a talented star. Individuals who were unlikely to be famous were made so through rock and roll. Many have died at 27 years of age.

Has the Devil been busy making more barters? Only those who have died, known as Club 27, know for sure. The list includes Jimi

Hendrix, Jim Morrison, and Kurt Cobain. All in all, there are 60 known members of Club 27.

And the music keeps playing.

# THERE'S SOMEONE IN THE HOUSE

### *October Twenty-Fifth*

Warner Martindale had a problem. His wife wouldn't let him sleep. In his job, he had to get up early to make contacts on east coast, then work his way west throughout the day. He was tired.

Being a salesman hadn't been easy on Jo Beth. There were long hours and there was travel. Lots of travel. Jo Beth had never liked it when he was away. If he hadn't been away as much, things may be a lot different.

Warner considered moving to a different neighborhood. One that was safer. His commissions never seemed to add up to more than the bills, though. Even living paycheck to paycheck would have been preferable.

Warner knew his wife had taken the worst of it. Oh, how he knew. She never let him forget it. But now, it seemed pointless to continue the argument.

He went to bed as always. He seemed to have slowly wafted into unconsciousness. Warner hadn't realized that he had fallen asleep.

"There's someone in the house," Jo Beth said.

Warner, a light sleeper anyways, sat up in bed. Jo Beth was pale. Her nightgown glowed in the moonlight coming through the open window. She looked terrified.

"Nobody is here, Jo Beth. Please, let me sleep," Warner pleaded.

"There's someone in the house," Jo Beth insisted.

Warner knew he wouldn't be able to go back to sleep unless he checked. He went through the motions of looking in the guest room, bathroom, and kitchen. He checked the newly-installed deadbolt and locks. There was no evidence of an intruder.

Warner went back to bed. He paid the price for the lack of sleep the next day. His game was off and he didn't get many sales. He really hoped he could catch up on sleep. That was all he really needed. To sleep and just forget all this prowler stuff.

Yet that night, it was the same. Warner had just fallen asleep when his wife woke him. "There is someone in the house," she said.

In fact, it had been like that every night Warner slept at home. Ever since Jo Beth had been murdered by the burglar. His wife wouldn't let him sleep.

# HEART OF STONE

## *October Twenty-Sixth*

The girl in the red petticoat and hair to match had waited almost four years for the chance to ask the handsome man to marry her. It was only proper on the leap year, she knew. If he was half the gentleman she knew him to be, he would not refuse her. His heart may have been made of stone, but he could not be so cold as to leave her a spinster.

It wasn't that she was unattractive. Quite the contrary. Many men had fawned over her through the years. She had just waited for the right man. For him. She had read about his heroism in the face of danger. He was a role model for all around him, yet soft spoken and modest.

He held his courage and valor as a regal steed carries itself, proud but not ostentatious. He was simultaneously modest and confident He was not at all like her father. How a prim and noble offspring could come from such degenerate stock was a mystery.

Her father, in name only, had only looked after himself. He never defended the weaker or worthy. In point of fact, he had exploited those unfortunate enough to fall prey to his treacherous exertions. She had not seen that growing up, but knew the painful truth as a result of her maturation. Had she only known now what she should have known then.

But no worry, her proverbial knight in shining armor would see to her every need after they were betrothed. He would stand up when she could not. Her husband would make right the wrongs that had been done to her over the years. And not just her father, she thought. Others would pay for their transgressions. She knew he would see to that. They would pay dearly.

She made her way to the front of the library where he stood stoically. Where he always remained. His sculpted, lifeless eyes stared out unseeingly at the world. She glanced around. Seeing that nobody was in sight, she stood on the pedestal. She stood on tiptoe to kiss his granite surface. "Will you be mine?" she asked.

The statue turned its head and nodded.

# MATRYOSHKA

## *October Twenty-Seventh*

The Russian State Security Committee was investigating a rash of deaths in the small town of Pryachetsya. One had been a field agent by the name of Fellah Kolstoy. Andrei Tolkarev was assigned to the case. He took a couple agents with him and set out for the countryside.

Once there, they had to meet with local police, a fat jovial man by the name of Oleg Morozov. Morozov tried to whitewash the events.

"You are all welcome. But these deaths. They are not suspicious. We had a warm winter and wet spring. Many deer were born. The wolf population grew, as well. I have men out to hunt them," Morozov explained.

His eyes darted frantically. Andrei could tell he was trying too hard. The man was lying.

"Lieutenant Morozov, we had a message from Agent Kolstoy. She described the town under some kind of superstitious hysteria. She said there was claims of monsters," Andrei said.

"Kolkhozniks. They see witches where there are merely wolves," Morozov said.

He winced, knowing he had said too much. "Witches?" Andrei asked.

"I know nothing of witches," Morozov said.

He laughed a mirthless chuckle. "We are getting nowhere. Let's talk with the landlord where Kolstoy lived," Andrei said.

"No!" Morozov objected.

"What?" Andrei asked.

"Not until you've eaten and rested," Morozov offered.

They left, threatening Morozov with obstruction if he interfered. At the edge of town, they found the boarding house.

It was on stilts, presumably to keep off the frozen ground. Andrei and his men went in. The stench hit them first.

They found a pot boiling in the fireplace as the source. Inside, were human limbs. The men drew their firearms.

The woman attacked from shadow. Her wail was inhuman. She had long fingernails and sharp teeth.

The men opened fire. The old woman was cut down instantly. "Morozov has some explaining to do," Andrei said.

They left, headed back to town.

From inside the old woman, something moved. Her flesh split apart. A smaller version of the witch emerged. She went to stir the pot. No sense letting the meal overcook.

Her stomach gurgled. "Now, sestra. Patience."

She patted her belly to calm her younger sibling.

## COPPER ANTS

### *October Twenty-Eighth*

The warehouse studio was overrun by the metallic monsters, scraping at the corrugated steel arcs which comprised the exterior of the building. Emmett and Kelvin barricaded the door while Kelvin's friend Sara grabbed more boxes from the shelves to bring to them. The windows were Plexiglas, luckily, and that may have bought them some time. None of the ants could break through it as easily as brittle glass.

"How many of those things did you make, Dad?" Kelvin asked.

Emmett pushed another box against the only door to the studio. If he could secure that, he thought, maybe they stood a chance. Maybe. "They are part of a series, Kel. I have been making them for twelve years. It's supposed to be a hive, but I put those things all over town as part of the display. The piece isn't finished yet, so I don't really know. Hundreds? Maybe thousands. It's been my masterpiece project for years. I've lost track."

Sara screamed. Emmett and Kelvin spun around. She was looking up at the skylights. Anthropoid shadows of many fabricated ant sculptures were strewn across the cement warehouse floor. Their giant forms mirrored the source as the creatures crawled about furiously trying to breach the divide.

"They are going to get in!" Sara yelled.

Emmett realized she was right. It was only a matter of minutes. "Quick," he said, "Grab my acetylene torch, Kel, and the mask. I am going to get a mallet. Sara, you run over to the loft and we will meet you up there."

Just as he gave the orders, one of the skylights gave way. A shower of plastic and metal hit the ground. Several copper ants followed, clanking loudly as they met the concrete forcefully. One broke apart, Emmett noticed, sending metal fragments flying. Others, though dented and bent, continued the assault.

"Run!" Emmett yelled.

Sara had already made it to the loft. Emmett ran to the back, away from the loft but towards his tools. He seized the large mallet and bolted back towards the loft. From the corner of his eye, he saw Kelvin running. He could only hope Kelvin had been able to grab the blow torch.

Emmett thought of the sheriff. Poor Sheriff Lumley, who shot six or seven 12 gauge rounds against the hordes. The shotgun blasts ineffectually ricocheted off the metallic surface of the ants as they charged him. The sheriff, who came to save them, was instead torn to small pieces by Emmett's animated artwork. His sculptures had somehow come alive.

Three copper ants scurried towards him. Emmett jumped over them like a champion pole-vaulter. He didn't even break stride as he sprinted towards the loft.

Emmett risked a glance over his shoulder to check on Kelvin, and was grateful he did. The boy was cornered by a half dozen of the little monsters. Kelvin met his father's eyes, fraught with terror.

"Dad!" Kelvin screamed for help.

"Behind you!" Sara warned.

Emmett spun around and saw that eight more ants had circled behind him. He ran towards Kelvin. Kelvin tried to smash one of the copper creatures with the oxygen tank from the torch he had snatched. It clunked, but the ant didn't succumb to the attack, instead writhing more angrily than before.

From the ceiling, copper ants continued to fall through the skylight to the floor. A few broke apart but the majority were able to join in the attack. The hoard was growing exponentially.

Making it to the boy in the nick of time, Emmett clobbered the closest ant with a wide swing of a mallet. The ant flew into metallic pieces. Others turned to attack Emmett, ignoring their initial prey.

From behind, they could hear the clinking of tiny metallic feet on the concrete floor. "Run, Kel. I will keep them on me!" Emmett ordered.

Kelvin objected, "But Dad!"

"Do it!" Emmett commanded.

Kelvin ran off, lugging the heavy torch and mask with him. Emmett turned to face the mass of the creatures. They had grouped together in force as they continued their attack.

It would only be a matter of seconds until they surrounded him, Emmett realized. That was how Sheriff Lumley died. Emmett couldn't let that happen. Once again, he vaulted over the charging ants and ran.

The front door gave way, sending various boxes falling backwards. The ants had broken through that way, too. Emmett glanced around, seeing that his progress to the loft was blocked by about sixty or seventy of the crawling nightmare. He wasn't going to make it, Emmett realized, with a sinking feeling in his gut.

Emmett backed up as the semicircle of now hundreds of ants closed in quickly. Ants he had fashioned himself from copper components he welded together. His mind reeled. Why was this happening? How?

Behind him, shelves of art supplies lined the walls. Emmett scanned the contents, trying to come up with a plan. He noticed several gallons of exterior enamel paint he had used on his studio. Tan, to help blend in with the mountainous surroundings of the desert. The cans had a little heft to them.

Emmett grabbed a nearly full gallon and threw it. It hit part of the swarm with little impact. He threw another, but the ants still advanced. The third burst open when it hit the floor in front. Paint gushed out.

The ants slipped in the paint, losing purchase on the floor with their copper feet. Emmett smiled as the idea came to him. He opened cans, pouring them in front. Ants slipped and scurried, spinning and getting momentarily stuck.

"Dad!" Kelvin screamed.

Emmett risked a glance towards the loft. Kelvin and Sara had found some rope, and were lowering it to the corner opposite the stairs. It was only about thirty feet away from Emmett. If he could reach it.

A sudden sting in his calf made Emmett cry out. He glanced down to see a two-foot long ant on his leg, its metal pinchers buried in his flesh. He flung the mallet down brushing the beast off hastily.

Blood poured from the wound. Ants began to crawl over the others writhing in the paint. They found their footing on the backs of the fallen and still advanced.

The painting supplies behind him also held a large plastic tarp. Emmett grabbed it, flinging it open. It was about twelve by fifteen feet. He threw it over the narrowest part of the encroaching swarm, covering them like he was making his bed. Underneath the sky-blue surface of the tarp the ants undulated wildly.

Emmett rolled over the ants, fearing he would trip if he tried to walk. It worked, and soon he was out of the corner. He ran, his calf screaming out in painful protest.

As the primary target, the swarm had all but ignored Kelvin and Sara but a few still blocked the stairs, climbing clumsily up the surface in an attempt to get at the kids. Emmett ran to the opposite side where the rope hung down.

Kelvin had tied the end to a support beam. Emmett stuck the mallet in his belt loop behind his back. He would need the large hammer, he knew. He couldn't afford to lose it now.

Emmett was grateful he kept in shape. Sheriff Lumley never would have been able to pull himself up. Climbing the rope was incredibly difficult, but he made it up as the swarm circled furiously beneath him.

Kelvin grabbed his father's hand, pulling him over the railing of the loft. They didn't bother withdrawing the rope as it hung four feet from the ground - way out of reach of the ants and thereby safe. The stairs were a different story.

Eight ants made it up the steps despite the difficult terrain for them. Emmett snatched the mallet from behind his back and charged. Sara kicked at one of the closest creatures. Its pincers clanked as it tried to seize her.

Emmett brought the mallet down hard on the ant. It exploded in large metal shards. Another ant snuck up from out of sight and sunk metal fangs into Emmett's hand. He screamed out in pain, dropping the mallet.

The hammer clanked down and tumbled, resting precariously on the edge of the loft floor. Kelvin ran to his father's rescue, sweeping the oxygen tank back and forth to knock the ants out of the way. More came up the stairs and onto the landing.

Sara grasped the mallet before one of the creatures knocked it over the side. She hammered at the ant, knocking it down to the concrete floor where it broke apart. She yelled in triumph.

The younger two fought against the ants. Emmett glanced around for a weapon. He found a push broom, which he used to literally sweep scores of the creatures off the landing, tumbling down the stairs. "We need to secure those stairs," Emmett said.

"How?" Kelvin asked.

"Bring me the mask and torch," Emmett replied.

Kelvin obliged, and Emmett made quick work of his chore despite a wounded calf and hand. He told the others to look away while he cut through the steel girders connecting the stairs. The loft was supported by two large beams and then bolted to the back of the warehouse. With a little effort, the stairwell fell with a cacophonous clatter to the ground below. They were trapped, but they had stopped the attack - for now.

The ants feverishly crawled about, trying to find a way to get at the three people on the landing. The walls were too slick and curved inward, making it impossible to climb as they had on the exterior surface. The beams were also too steep and smooth to permit the ants to ascend. The creatures massed beneath them, appearing as real ants from their height instead of two foot long metallic monsters.

Emmett was bleeding profusely from his calf and hand. Now that they could catch their breath, Kelvin, Sara, and even Emmett knew that they had to tend to those wounds. There was a genuine concern that Emmett could bleed to death.

There was a cot in the corner where Emmett would sleep when he sometimes pulled all-nighters. Kelvin grabbed the sheets and handed one end to Sara. "Tear off strips, Sare. We have to make some bandages. Dad, lie down," Kelvin said.

Emmett, weak from blood loss and the attack, merely nodded. He hobbled over to the cot, flopping down on the canvas surface. Kelvin took strips and wound them tightly around Emmett's leg and hand. Sara handed him more strips as he continued bandaging.

"This makes no sense. None at all. Why would this series come alive? How could it come alive? And why not anything else I have sculpted over the years. Why not the nice dolphin series I did in bronze? Or even the elephant...anything but ants," Emmett mumbled, almost incoherently.

Sara and Kelvin looked at each other, eyes filled with guilt. This exchange was not lost on Emmett. "What do you two know?" he asked.

"Nandid Chopra," Kelvin whispered.

"You've lost me," Emmett said.

Sara explained, "He was an alchemist from three hundred years ago. Folks said he sold his soul to the devil for the power of transmutation. Well, that's what we thought anyway."

Emmett stared at Sara as if she had gone insane. He looked at his son quizzically. "It's true, Dad. Sort of," Kelvin said.

"What do you mean 'sort of'?" Sara asked.

"Well," Kelvin said, "It wasn't exactly Satan. It was Kali. An Indian demon. Nandid was from India, after all."

"Demons are demons, Kel. He still sold his soul to the devil no matter what name you give it. We never should have messed around with it. It is evil," Sara argued.

"Wait, wait wait. Start at the beginning. I am so confused right now," Emmett said.

Kelvin continued, "Nandid Chopra was an alchemist, like Sara said. He had an amulet that was the source of his powers. It was this small vial inside a gold pendant of twisting snakes. The vial holds the blood of Kali."

"The amulet is magic," Sara explained.

Emmett thought of discounting the ridiculous notion. The sound of hundreds of copper ants scurrying about in his studio quickly quashed his retort, however. He urged the children to continue. "How did you get it?" Emmett asked.

"You sent me down to the pawn shop to get some raw materials for your artwork. I got all the metal I could find, bronze, steel, copper, and gold. That piece was one of the things someone had pawned. Can you believe it?" Kelvin said.

"How do you know all about it, then, if you just bought it? The pawn shop owner?" Emmett asked.

"No," Sara said, "that was where I came in. Kel gave me the pendant as a kind of...well..."

"I asked her to be my girlfriend," Kelvin stated.

Sara blushed. "Anyway, I thought it was beautiful, but also a little weird. I did some research. I found it on an image search of the web. I figured out all about Nandid Chopra and told Kel."

Kelvin said, "And we figured we would test it out."

"Test it out?" Emmett asked.

"His alchemy. Transmutation. Turning lead into gold. Or, copper into gold, in this case," explained Kelvin.

Emmett shook his head and closed his eyes tightly. He lay back, sighing deeply. "This is crazy," he said.

"So," Sara continued, "we broke open the vial of blood. It seemed to work, but obviously Kali must have cursed the amulet. We never should have messed around with it, Kel."

Kelvin replied, "I know you're right, Sare. But it might have been amazing. We could all have been set for life."

"You poured the blood onto all of those ants trying to turn them into gold?" Emmett asked.

"No, just one. It worked, too...until it came alive," Kelvin said.

"What happened?" Emmett asked.

Kelvin said, "We poured it on one of your sculptures, which changed. Then it came alive - and all the rest of that series of your artwork."

Emmett realized what Kelvin was saying with horror. Just as it dawned on him, he heard a loud crash and creak of tearing metal as the west wall caved in. The three of them ran to the railing of the loft to investigate.

The crowning centerpiece of years of work walked around on its six gigantic metal legs. Though Emmett had sculpted it out of copper, it was now gleaming gold in composition.

The sculpture was as big as a dump truck, and until recently had been standing in the city park where Emmett had donated it. The golden queen ant entered the studio, tearing through all obstacles in its path. It scrambled towards the loft, followed by hundreds of its faithful servants.

The swarm attacked, led by the golden queen, who easily tore through the steel girders supporting the loft. Right before they fell, Emmett whispered, "I really wish you would have tried the amulet out on the dolphin sculpture, instead."

# SINS OF THE FATHER

### *October Twenty-Ninth*

Rory Fennel Jr. knew his way around an automobile. He had grown up in his father's repair shop, learning the trade. The U-Pick junkyard was where he pieced out crashed vehicles to fix cars in his own shop. Then, he upped the price of the parts over three hundred percent. He could even charge new prices for the used parts. The customers were too clueless to know the difference.

Rory had made a deal with the owners to come in after close. He paid a little more to do so, but his repeat business was what really sealed the deal. It was a good system.

Now, he wanted the starter from a 1982 Lincoln Continental. The valor and dignity once personified in the vehicle was reduced to twisted metal. But the engine block was mostly intact. At least, the starter was.

Rory worked on loosening the rusted bolts. Rory leaned back, looking up at the night sky. Clouds rolled by slowly. It was very quiet and relaxing in the junkyard after dark.

It didn't stay quiet, though. Soon, a low moaning sound steadily rose. Rory looked up.

There, a ghastly apparition stood. It was luminescent blue and only slightly opaque. It was dressed in a ragged chauffeur's uniform. The man was bruised and cut. Teeth shown through a torn cheek.

"You did this," blamed the specter.

He said, "I'm just getting a part. You're in a junkyard."

"You did this," it repeated.

"Why do you think I did this?" Rory asked.

"Are you Rory Fennel?" asked the apparition.

Rory nodded. "Yes, but,"

The ghost interrupted, "Then you did this. You fixed the Lincoln with shoddy parts. As a result, I crashed on the highway and died. You did this."

The Lincoln Continental was over thirty years old. Rory had been a child at the time. His father, though. It must have been Rory Fennel Senior that worked on the Lincoln.

Before he could correct the misunderstanding, the ghost enveloped him. Rory's hair turned white instantly. He would never work on another car again. In fact, he would never say another word again. He would just stare out blankly knowing what the afterlife had in store.

# THE GHOST WHO SOLVED HER OWN MURDER

### *October Thirtieth*

It would have been the perfect crime. Edward Shue was a man prone to fits of rage. His young newlywed of a scant three months would find that out by strangulation. Edward was able to cover up the murder quite adeptly. Or so he thought.

The incident took place in Greenbriar County, West Virginia. The body of his lifeless bride, Zona Heaster Shue, was discovered by a young lad at the foot of the stairs where Edward had thrown it. He went to tell the authorities.

Edward had since taken the body upstairs and dressed her in a high, stiff collared dress to hide the bruises on her neck. He placed a veil over her face and played the part of the grieving widower well. The coroner who examiner Zona Heaster was convinced.

He ruled the death as coronary failure. Zona Heaster was buried and that seemed to be the end of it. But, it wasn't. Not by far.

Mary Jane Heaster, Zona's mother, received the real story of the murder. It came from an unlikely source. Zona Heaster herself.

The spectral apparition visited Mary Jane for four nights. Each haunting grew progressively worse with the description of the horrific event. Finally, Mary Jane could take no more and went to the authorities with the news. Her daughter had been murdered.

Mary Jane convinced them to exhume Zona Heaster's remains and examine them for foul play. Edward Shue vehemently opposed this, which seemed to work against him. He revealed his potential fury, leading the police to consider that his wife was murdered.

An autopsy revealed the cause of death. Edward was arrested. He died in prison, despite an attempt by an angry mob to lynch him.

Today, a Greenbriar historical plaque marks the gravesite of Zona Heaster Shue. It reads:

"Interred in nearby cemetery is Zona Heaster Shue. Her death in 1897 was presumed natural until her spirit appeared to her mother to describe how she was killed by her husband Edward. Autopsy on the exhumed body verified the apparition's account. Edward, found guilty of murder, was sentenced to the state prison. Only known case in which testimony from a ghost helped convict a murderer."

## SMOKE DANCER

### *October Thirty-First*

The miscreants of Saint Rose Philippine Duchesne High decided to go camping over Halloween weekend. Their classification was somewhat of a misnomer seeing as it was designated by Sister Fowler. To her, anyone who did not have the 23rd Psalm memorized was a qualifying member. In reality, their bark was very much more than their bite.

At Rosie High, the nickname given by those miscreants, it was teacher planning on Friday the 31st. This meant an extra day off from classes. The holiday provided an excuse to hang out together outside of the protective confines of teachers, nuns, and parents. In the case of Carl Maldonado it was all three.

He was the de facto leader of the group now that Manny Ortiz had been expelled. Worse, Manny had been shipped off to some distant military academy. They had written him off from being in the group since he was unlikely ever to see the sunlight over Rosie High again. Carl stepped in and filled his shoes, even if he had to deceive his mother from time to time to pull it off.

Carl had them all meet at Lovelake Cemetery, parking in the visitor area away from Main Street so as not to be noticed by any potential buzz-kills. The graveyard was walking distance from the high school. Regardless, they all drove.

This was their last year. They would soon graduate and friendships would naturally dissolve, Carl thought. Sometimes, Carl felt like his high school friends were closer to him than his own family. But, he also knew that these friendships were fickle. Like Manny Ortiz. Out of sight, out of mind.

Still, Carl held a tenuous grasp on the group. He planned to for as long as possible. He knew things were inevitably changing.

They were the class of 1987, set to walk the next year. Well, mostly. All except for Lelia Hatathli, that was. She was only fifteen and didn't even have a learner's permit yet. They let her into the group because she was cute but she was still a newcomer. Lelia bummed a ride from Alexis Garner. Rounding out the group were Lloyd Tabaaha, Rene Peshlakai, Dwayne Billings, and Javier Gomez. Three girls and four boys. Almost someone for everyone, though none of them were official couples as of yet.

Their life together was measured by a scant half semester. Javier was moving to Piñon so he could work in his aunt's dry cleaning business full time. Lloyd and Rene were both going to the community college in Cortez, then Rene was even planning on attending Colorado Mesa University for a nursing degree after she was done with her generals. Alexis might stay, but wasn't too keen on it. Lelia still had a couple years but had already talked about going to Denver. Dwayne was definitely a Juniper lifer. And then there was Carl.

Carl was secretly terrified he couldn't leave. He didn't even have plans after high school. He felt trapped. What was worse than being stuck in Juniper all your life? Carl knew that would be Dwayne's fate. Trapped in some meaningless job washing cars or slinging burgers. Carl wanted more. He knew there were places out there beyond the broadcast reach of the town's only piss-ant little country AM radio station. He feared that he wasn't strong enough to make it, though. Something he could never admit to anyone. What if he wasn't good enough to leave?

And all he had to show for his nearly four years of high school were the friends he had made. Seeing that dissolve was terrifying. Or worse, not being able to give up his high school persona at all.

He would be like those creepy dudes in their twenties who went to high school parties uninvited. People let them in because they could buy beer, but they never truly let them in. To Carl, that was a fate worse than death.

He tried to push all the worry and insecurity out of his mind. Make this party epic, he thought. Focus on that. It was nearly time. Better to forge memories than to miss opportunities.

Lovelake Cemetery was surrounded by large, stately cottonwoods which nearly secluded the place from view off the main road. Six cars for seven people. It looked like a wake. "We're going to attract some unwanted attention with all these cars," Rene said.

Rene was the pragmatic one of the group. She was also bordering on annoying. Sometimes, it was like having another Sister Fowler around. Or worse, Carl's mother and Algebra II teacher, Mrs. Maldonado. Heaven forbid.

"Ain't nobody gonna see these cars where we parked them. If anyone does see, they will just make the sign of the cross, mumble and rub their rosaries and drive on. Plus, cops will have enough to do with all the Devil's Night pranks. We can take Dwayne's truck and all fit in the bed. I ride shotgun, of course," said Carl.

"You always get shotgun," complained Lloyd.

Carl replied, "I called it squares, dude."

They compiled whatever gear they thought to bring in the back of the truck along with everyone except for Carl and Dwayne, who rode in the cab of the old Ford. Dwayne revved the engine loudly and they took off with a start.

Kids flew backward and rolled around in the bed amongst Dwayne's baseball gear, oily rags, some old beer cans, and other assorted trash. Carl laughed and Dwayne nodded a cool head bob as acknowledgement.

Camping was a loose term for their plans. Dwayne had a case of Pabst Blue Ribbon on ice in an utterly thrashed Igloo cooler, Alexis had pinched a fifth of scotch from her grandfather, Lloyd had some tequila, and even Carl contributed with a bag of weed his sister had scored for him from a friend in Cortez. Nobody had considered bringing food or water. Even sleeping bags had been an afterthought.

The camping was going to consist of getting wasted and hopefully make it a few bases or even all the way. Carl could only hope. Secretly, he just wished he wasn't the odd man out.

"Where we going? Usual party place?" Dwayne asked.

"No," Carl said, "I think we're going to go a little bit more away from people this weekend. Drive towards Yellow Jacket. There's an old ranch access road that crosses through the desert. Place I'm thinking about is just past there."

Dwayne nodded. "What's up there, dude?"

"It's in BLM land," Carl replied.

"What's that?"

"Bureau of Land Management," Carl said.

Dwayne shrugged in confusion. Carl explained, "It's public land. Free camping. Dude, you are so stupid sometimes."

"Sorry, I don't know nothing about no places. I ain't no geology major," Dwayne said.

Carl said, "Geography, you mean."

Dwayne rolled his eyes. "You could have just said 'free camping spots' or 'desert' or something 'stead of playing all Poindexter," he muttered.

The boy's face contorted into a pout, brows furrowed and eyes narrowed. He grew stiff, concentrating on nothing but the road. Carl had hurt his feelings. Dwayne was a loyal friend, but he was as dumb as a sock drawer full of shoelaces. On the other hand, he had a big truck. It sure came in handy for situations such as this, Carl thought.

"Sorry, dude. No more school talk. So, which one you going to take a crack at back there, huh?" Carl said, changing the subject.

Dwayne checked the rear view mirror. "That Lelia girl is tight," he said.

Carl laughed. "Dude, she is fifteen. And you're almost eighteen. Going to send you to jail, that will. 'sides, I thought you and Rene were a thing."

"I tried," Dwayne confided, "but she played the friend card."

"Bummer," said Carl.

"What, you like Lelia? You want to keep her for yourself? Is that what you mean?" Dwayne asked.

"No," Carl replied, "I like Alexis. I think she likes me too. I'm going to get really smashed and try to find out."

"Good plan, dude."

"Then we can let Lloyd and Javier fight it out over Rene," Carl joked.

They drove in silence for a while, each admiring the vast unspoiled desert surrounding them. The sun stretched the shadows into long spindly fingers across the highway as the sun lowered in the horizon.

"Roll down the windows and crank some tunes. That's the turnoff up ahead on the left," Carl said.

Dwayne obliged, even pulling back the sliding rear window. Hoots and hollers of encouragement came from the passengers in the bed of the truck. Carl suspected that maybe they hadn't waited to start partaking in the party supplies.

Dwayne barely slowed down on the dirt road, though the surface was eroded and jetting with stones. At one bump, Carl's head flew backwards. He hit part of the empty hard plastic gun rack mounted to the rear window. "Ouch! Dude?" Carl complained.

The bodies in the back bounced, as well. Many clamored to hold onto something. Miraculously, nobody dropped the tequila bottle. Finally, Rene yelled, "Slow down!"

Dwayne laughed at her, but he slowed down nonetheless. Carl turned around to see the rest of the group. As he thought, they had opened the bottle of tequila. It looked like half the contents were getting spilled with the bumpy road, but many took healthy swigs as they passed it around.

Except for Lelia. She was putting on a good show, but even from the cab of the truck Carl could see that she was only holding the bottle to her lips and pursing them closed as she tipped it back for effect. The young girl hadn't even thought to pretend to swallow.

"I was right, Dwayne. They are getting hammered back there," Carl said.

Dwayne laughed. "Hey man," he said, "it's back of the truck privilege. Has to be some perks to riding there."

Carl laughed. "I guess you're right. Is that your soiled underwear back there?" he said.

Dwayne had to check. "Naw, man. Some old socks. I used them to check the oil. Now those, in the corner, those are my dirty drawers."

They laughed. They soon found a suitable spot to pull off the road. The place was filled with natural red rock structures with very little plant life at all. It felt like they were on the surface of Mars, billions of miles away from everyone else.

It was Halloween eve. They were free. And the entire world was theirs. If only for a brief moment.

***

The smell of burning ironwood and sage filled their nostrils. The pleasant odor was cleansed only by another drink of beer or scotch. The tequila was long gone.

That was until they lit up a joint. Then, the only smell was the stench of the small blunt smothering out the remainder of the nicer aroma. Carl took the first hit.

If his mother could only see him now, he thought. He laughed, coughing, as he passed the smoke to Dwayne. In short order the tiny amount of marijuana was literally up in smoke.

But the weed and alcohol had done their job. Even Lelia looked altered, though Carl figured it was just a contact high. She was still faking it like a poser, he noticed.

"Canyon of the Ancients, man," Carl said.

They all nodded like they knew what he was talking about. For a second, Carl figured they did for nobody prompted him to continue. He watched the cotton candy clouds drift by lazily, flavored by the setting sun.

"Right, Lloyd?" Carl asked.

Lloyd's eyes were mere slivers. He was feeling no pain. Lloyd didn't respond.

Carl repeated, "Right, Lloyd?"

After a slight hesitation, Lloyd said, "Whatever you say, man."

He giggled.

"Yeah, Canyon of the Ancients," Carl repeated.

He got up and threw some more twigs and branches on the flames. The stump they had found would burn all night if they kept it going, Carl knew. Once it got hot enough, that was.

He tended the fire, poking it with a long stick. Without saying a word, Carl was begging for someone to ask what he meant by his intentionally cryptic comment. At last, Alexis took the bait. "What is the Canyon of the Ancients, Carl?" she asked.

Carl relished the moment. He approached her, as if invited, sitting closely. She didn't back away. That was a good sign, he thought.

He considered putting an arm around her as he began the story, but decided he might need a little more liquid courage before going that far. He took a swig of scotch, feeling it burn down his throat and settle warmly in his chest. "Canyon of the Ancients. We are smack dab right in the middle of it, folks."

"Cool," Javier said.

Carl continued, "Those looming columns of rocks. When the sun goes down, like it will soon, they lose all their color and definition. They look like people. Shadows standing around you in the distance."

Rene replied, "Yeah, they kind of do, don't they. Especially those over there. If you kind of squint your eyes, you can see that one is a fat woman and the other is a short dude. Three ones over there-"

Carl cut her off, knowing that Rene would steal his spotlight if he let her. "Yes, they look like people watching us. Silently. But knowing all the legends of these parts. The tales. The awful, bloody tales. Tales almost forgotten by us mere people."

"What tales?" asked Lelia.

Carl smiled sardonically. "Of the horrors, true horrors, that plague these desolate mountains, ravines, flatlands, and canyons. Things like the skinwalkers. Or the chupacabra. Wendigo. Tshakapesh. Owl-witches and lychanthrope. Ghosts, curses, and monsters. Tales to turn your hair white and dry the mouth."

"Dude, I'm going to have dry mouth tomorrow from this hooch," said Dwayne.

"Tell us about one, Carl," Alexis urged.

Lelia added, "Yeah, tell us a ghost story."

Carl tried to maintain his composure. This was going better than he had hoped. With any luck, he was laying the groundwork to pair off before the night was over. He swallowed. His nose had begun to tingle from the alcohol.

"There's one, right there," he pointed.

The six others looked to where he directed. There was nothing there, of course. "Ha, made you look," said Javier.

"No," Carl objected, "really. Right there."

"All I see is the campfire," Rene said.

"Exactly. Well, the smoke to be more precise," Carl stated.

"The smoke? Dude, you're were smoking it all right," said Javier as he leaned back on the ground.

Carl laughed. "You're right, but that doesn't change the fact that you're looking at a ghost in that column of smoke. A demon ghost."

"Awesome," Lloyd said with his eyes entirely closed now.

Alexis asked, "What do you mean, Carl?"

This time, he did place an arm around her. She didn't shrug it off. His confidence now completely bolstered, Carl began his tale without further prompting.

"My grandfather was a Mescalero Apache. Mom called him Pete but his real name was Running Breeze. I called him Breaking Wind," said Carl.

Several laughed.

"He was kind of a nut, but he knew a lot of the oral traditions. Stories. Stuff that was never written down because they didn't have a written language when he was young.

"He had all kinds of strange stories of monsters and curses and the like. I thought they were stupid when I was young. As I grew older, I found out that they weren't just made up.

"One of the stories he told me was about a demon ghost here in the Canyon of the Ancients. He called it the hún'bú'cé."

"The butt-munch, you say?" Dwayne joked.

Carl smiled, but didn't laugh. He continued, "It means smoke dancer in Mescalero. Never written down and almost never spoken aloud since my grandfather was a boy. He said I was the first half-breed ever to learn the word at all."

"Half breed?" asked Javier.

"Grandfather didn't like the fact that my father was Mexican. Said it weakened the bloodline," Carl explained.

"Dude, that's rude!" Javier replied, sitting up in protest.

"It's okay. He loved me. He said the Apache blood had eaten up all the Mexican blood in me," Carl said.

Javier actually stood at this point, which was no small feat in his condition. "That is just wrong, man. What the hell?"

"Yeah, what the hell?" Lloyd agreed through slurred speech.

Carl waved a hand, trying to calm his friend down. "I didn't say I believed that crap. I just said my grandfather did. I am proud to be half-Mexican, bro."

"That's better," Javier said and sat again.

Lelia replied, "My grandparents are the same way. Only they are Pueblo."

"It's a generational thing," said Alexis, "My grandparents think I should only date whites."

With that, she nuzzled closer to Carl in defiant rebellion of her grandparents. Carl actually closed his eyes and sighed.

Rene giggled.

"But back to the story. The hún'bú'cé. The Smoke Dancer. It isn't actually the smoke. It lives in the smoke. When the fire awakens it, the column of smoke is the house. Get it?" Carl asked.

A few people nodded. Rene said, "Totally."

"What does it do, Carl?" asked Alexis.

"I am so glad you asked, Alexis. Let me tell you. It chooses a bride," he said.

"Righteous," said Dwayne.

"Or a groom. It can be man or woman, depending on who it chooses to marry. Once it decides, it comes out of the smoke and into the person as one being. That person is then the physical embodiment of the smoke demon.

"Then, once it has human form, it has to eat. It needs the flesh of other people so it can stay in the host body. Wicked, huh?" Carl beamed.

Lloyd had passed out and began to snore. Carl feared he might lose his audience. He picked it up again before the pause turned into a full lull.

"But I didn't tell you how it chooses a bride or groom, did I? Come, let's circle the fire closely and I will explain," he enticed.

All but Lloyd made a circle around the flames. The column of smoke rose languidly towards the heavens. Carl smiled.

"Do we have to hold hands, say magic words, or dance or anything?" asked Rene.

"Naw, that's stupid. We don't have to do anything but wait. Once the hún'bú'cé has decided, it will show us who it picked."

"How?" Lelia asked.

"The smoke will turn. It will begin to dance. Move around. Then, it will bend down and touch us. If it stays on a person for more than a few seconds, then we know it has decided," said Carl.

"The Smoke Dancer," Alexis said with reverence.

"What happens if that person is already married," asked Dwayne.

"You have something to tell us, dude?" Javier asked.

They laughed.

"Naw, just figured it would only have one bride. Unless it was in Utah, that is," Dwayne said.

More laughter.

"I don't know. All I know is that aside from me and my grandfather, you guys are the first to hear this story in many, many decades. Maybe even a hundred years. Kind of makes us all special now, don't it?" asked Carl.

They stood in silence for a while, actually feeling honored by Carl sharing the story. Except for sleeping Lloyd, that was. Carl felt proud.

"Can we sit down and wait, Carl?" asked Rene.

"Yeah, dude, my dogs are barking," said Javier.

Carl replied, "I don't see why not. Smoke dancer will choose one of us sooner or later. We might as well get comfy."

They all plopped down on the rocky ground, still encircling the campfire. Carl sat close enough to Alexis that they could hold hands. Something she had initiated herself.

None spoke for a long time, awaiting the Smoke Dancer's decision. The sun finally set completely, kicking up the land breeze with the changing temperature. With that, the smoky column began to move. "Finally," Javier said.

The smoky tendrils blew softly, at first. Indirectly swirling around. Tufts of smoke gently caressed their faces briefly. With each pass, whomever it touched laughed or said something sardonic. The smoke didn't remain on anyone for very long.

"Maybe it's looking for a virgin," Dwayne mocked.

"Good luck with that," said Javier.

They all laughed again.

The wind grew bolder, swaying the smoke even further. Soon, it washed past them, sweeping their shoulders and chests. Rene coughed.

"Does that mean I'm the one?" she hacked.

"It didn't stay on you," said Alexis.

"Oh, you always think you're the prettiest," Rene complained.

"This isn't a beauty contest," Alexis replied.

The two girls sparred verbally for a moment until Javier finally cut them off. "Shut up!" he yelled.

"Speaking of rude," Rene complained.

"No," Javier yelled, "I mean it! Look! There! Look at Lelia!"

Everyone had been so focused on the catfight that nobody noticed what was happening to the young girl. She was enveloped in a smoky embrace, billowy tentacles wrapped around her. Her dark hair flew wildly about as if it had become flames. Her eyes had turned completely white. Veins pulsed through her face and neck. Then, she began to rise.

She was twenty feet off the ground before anyone was able to shake themselves out of the stupor. Alexis was first, pulling Carl by the shirt as she encouraged him to move. "We have to get out of here!" she yelled.

Carl nodded. They ran. He finally realized that the Smoke Dancer had chosen its bride.

***

Carl and Alexis ran directly opposite of the truck. They were facing northeast and it was the path of least resistance for them. Instinct had taken over and they fled without thought.

Rene took off to the northwest, not realizing that there were sheer cliffs not too far off. She ran, screaming. Blind panic guided her, which also led her right to a small ironwood stump. She tripped over it, tumbling over right to the edge of the precipice. It was enough to clear her head for a moment.

Javier was stunned and remained by the campfire. Lelia saw him with her pupil-less white eyes. Her head cocked and she smiled revealing jagged, impossibly long teeth. Instead of standing on her feet she floated on a writhing plume of smoke, gently bobbing up and down as if adrift on the ocean.

It was at this moment that Lloyd finally woke up from all the clamor. He stood and saw Lelia hovering over Javier. "Man," Lloyd said, "I'm trippin' hardcore. I need some water or something."

Lelia spun towards Lloyd. She cackled a hollow, echoed laugh. She floated towards him.

Dwayne ran for the truck. Javier ran towards it, as well. Javier was first, but he wasn't getting in the cab. He grabbed the aluminum baseball bat from the truck bed and ran back towards Lelia.

Dwayne got into the truck. He pumped the gas pedal frantically as he turned over the key. The truck refused to start. He had flooded the engine. Dwayne pounded on the dash with his fists in frustration.

Lelia was on Lloyd before he could realize he wasn't hallucinating. He began to scream from the attack, though it didn't last long. She tore at his neck with her ragged, nasty long teeth. Her fingernails grew into snake-like needles, curled and dripping with ichor. They plunged into his flesh, pumping and sucking as they drew blood and fluids from his body. He began to wither like a sun-dried tomato before their eyes.

Javier ran to help, swinging the bat violently. It hit Lloyd's body first, freeing it from Lelia's grasp. It fell to the stony earth below without even so much as a thud.

Javier pulled back and aimed for her head. The swing was powerful and Lelia didn't retreat from the hit. It struck the young girl in the temple and jaw, actually knocking her head cockeyed gruesomely. Javier didn't wait, but swung again stronger. This time, the head did come off and rolled away for a moment before exploding into a puff of smoke.

It was like a bizarre magic act. One minute the bludgeoned, decapitated head of the Lelia-demon was sneering up at them and the next it had evaporated into smoke. Then, Carl noticed the hovering headless body.

The neck spit forth a plume as it if were on fire. The smoke gathered, growing more and more opaque as it took the form of Lelia's head once again. It grew back, eyes wide and teeth barred.

She growled.

With a smack from the back of her hand, Javier went flying backwards a good ten feet or so. The baseball bat fell from his hands with a metallic clang.

The lower half of Lelia's body lost shape and definition, changing to smoke. The demon girl reared up like a cobra. Her hands grew to facilitate longer, thicker snake-tooth fingernails. Talons.

The thing swooped down as if she were a rattler, striking at Javier's prostrate body. The boy never recovered. She began to drain him as she had done with Lloyd and soon the boy was unrecognizable.

Rene screamed, though Carl and Alexis couldn't see from behind the roaring campfire. Lelia turned to her, rising above the peaks of the flames for a better vantage point. Suddenly, an explosion rang out and a gaping hole emerged in Lelia's torso.

Carl instinctually covered his ears. His mouth went agape. He turned to his left to see Dwayne, shotgun in his hands.

"I forgot I put it under the seat while I am in school," he said, smiling.

Lelia turned, the hole in her middle filling with smoke before turning back into her body again. She sneered at Dwayne.

"We have to run, Carl! We have to run and hide now!" Alexis demanded.

She pulled his arm with all her might, making Carl stumble backwards. His gaze was fixated on the confrontation, though, and he would not be swayed so easily.

Dwayne pumped the action and fired another round from the shotgun into Lelia's throat. Instead of blood splatter, Carl noticed it was sparks and smoke that came out of the girl like what happens when you throw a new long onto a campfire. She began to attack Dwayne.

Though he fired three more shotgun rounds into the approaching form, each wound miraculously transformed from smoke and back into flesh before their eyes. A swipe of a talon-clawed hand raked across his face, puncturing an eyeball and splitting the nose.

Dwayne gasped in shock before the girl was biting and tearing into his flesh. Carl could actually hear the sucking noises from her fingernails as they drew in fluids greedily. Alexis let go of Carl's arm and ran.

Carl didn't hesitate, tearing out after the girl as she ran quickly through the darkness. Rene screamed again, a distant sound that echoed through the canyons.

The Lelia monster dropped Dwayne to the ground and turned towards the screaming girl. Rene's eyes darted around quickly, plotting any potential escape. At the end of the Cliffside, there was none. She was trapped.

Lelia rose again, arched over the fire, and wafted towards Rene. Rene quit screaming, her mouth gasping for breath as she hyperventilated from fear. Lelia approached slowly. The hunter was in no hurry.

Seeing the inevitable coming, Rene decided for another option. She stood, looking down the cliff. Through the rising gloom of night, she couldn't see the rocks below. She knew they were there, though.

She took a step back towards Lelia so she would be able to have a running start. Rene ran to the edge. And she jumped.

Lelia wasn't having it. The creature turned into a wispy long coil of smoke and darted towards her plummeting victim. The smoke curled around the girl's neck and solidified.

The smoke turned into a rope, pulling Rene up and back to the top of the cliff. The girl struggled and clawed at her throat, desperate for air.

Rene's eyes bulged and her vision blurred. Once she was atop the rock, the noose loosened. Rene took a deep breath. Two. Three and then Lelia was on the attack once again.

The thing didn't like carrion. Lelia wanted live prey. It fed on Rene, who was soon lifeless and drained like the others.

Carl and Alexis kept running. It seemed like they had run for hours, when in actuality it had only been a few minutes. They stopped to catch their breath.

"Do you think it can find us?" Alexis gasped.

Carl shook his head, not in the negative but to indicate he didn't have a clue. His lungs felt like they would burst. They eventually recovered and set out in the same direction – away from camp. This time, though, they walked.

Coyotes howled in the night. Crickets chirped. They could hear the soft breeze through the underbrush.

It was a moonless night and soon clouds robbed them of the starlight that had been their only illumination. Twice, Carl had twisted his ankle and once Alexis actually tripped over a bush. Far away lightning sparked behind an outcropping of rocks. The flash silhouetted the Canyon of the Ancients, only witnesses to the carnage of their legends.

"We have to find a place to hide, Carl," Alexis said.

"A cave. There are caves at the base of the Ancients. We head for where they were just illuminated and we should find them," Carl said.

They changed course and headed to the large, columnar rocks. More yips in quick succession alluded to the fact that the coyotes had caught their prey. There was no sign of Lelia, though they could see a tiny glowing orb in the distance where the campfire still burned.

Carl could smell rain. The angry night sky also threatened a storm. "We'd better hurry," he said.

Despite the risk of spraining an ankle or even breaking a leg, they jogged once again. The land grew flat as they headed through the bottom of the ravine towards the Ancients, spurring them on even quicker. They ran.

They were soon there and shortly after that, they had found a small cave. More of an indentation, really, but somewhere out of sight nonetheless. They felt safe, nestled in the bosom of one of the Ancients.

The rains came shortly thereafter. At first, loud droplets spattered against the rocks in modest percussion. Soon, the sky opened up and the downpour began.

The once-distant lightning had also grown close, accompanied almost immediately by riotous thunder. Carl and Alexis huddled together, sitting on the ground.

"If this ravine floods, we'll drown in a flash flood. Look, that arroyo is beginning to run already," Alexis said.

Carl craned his neck to see the wash between flashes of lighting. The water was running swiftly, he could see. With the rocks and low saturation of the sand, runoff was almost immediate in such quick desert storms.

"We could climb up to-" Carl began.

He didn't finish. In the next lightning flash, Lelia was there. She had found them.

Shockingly, Lelia spoke in a raspy, demonic voice. She said, "Did you really think I wouldn't find you? Worse, did you really think the Ancients would conspire with you and betray me? Foolish prey. No, they told me exactly where you were hiding!"

The creature arched back on the serpentine body of smoke that supported her torso. Her arms grew and hands splayed outward as the fingernails coiled into talons. Her mouth grew apart and her jaw unhinged as more teeth emerged from bloody gums.

She wailed in anger, poised for attack.

Then, Lelia began to twitch in pain. Small poofs of smoke spurted from her body in many places. The column of smoke supporting her evaporated and she fell to her human legs on the slick surface of the rock below. She went down on her knees, arms covering her head.

Lelia shook her head. "No!" she cried out.

"Look!" Alexis pointed.

From their camp, the fire was sputtering and dying. The rain was extinguishing it.

As it fluttered and died, Lelia began to turn into smoke entirely. Quickly, even that dissipated into the running torrents. A hollow wail faded, drown out by the storm.

The campfire had gone out.

***

They made it back to camp. Over time, the excess gasoline had evaporated and the engine was no longer flooded. This time the old

Ford started. The two of them drove back towards town, briefly discussing just what they would tell people.

They were desperate to find a cover story to explain the deaths of their friends in a way that wouldn't implicate them or make them seem insane. It didn't really matter, though, Carl thought. Sooner or later there would be another campfire. Somewhere. It was inevitable.

And from those flames would rise the Smoke Dancer.

# SKELETON CREW

### *November First*

The arrangement had been simple. In exchange for "manning" a spacecraft that didn't need to bog itself down with atmospheric generators, rations, or other cumbersome cargo that had little return on investment for scientific discovery, Mishenka Belov would pilot the spacecraft. A living being would have been a liability. Mishenka hadn't been a living being since the space race in the late fifties.

After the fall of the USSR, SynTech acquired Mishenka's "remains". The undead cosmonaut's exploration into the realms of space and subsequently alternate reality proved interesting to the megacorporation. Especially the cosmic radioactive dust that reanimated Mishenka's corpse.

Such ventures are rarely built on a foundation of trust. This is where the relationship crumbled. Mishenka knew of SynTech's treacherous history. SynTech didn't trust communists. This became evident when Mishenka had tried to deviate from the flight plan.

Subroutines within the navigation system automatically course-corrected. Mishenka was at the mercy of autopilot. This would have been less troublesome had the debris not been directly in his path.

Pieces of some past man-made craft were often stuck in geosynchronous orbit, but something set them off target. Perhaps a speck of dust. Maybe a solar flare. Perhaps the moon phase. Regardless, the rocket struck metal, simultaneously knocking out engine #1 and throwing the spacecraft off trajectory.

Mishenka tried to compensate by blowing the second engine in bursts. He knew that he may be able to spin around until he corrected the error. That was when the second piece of debris knocked out engine #2.

Mishenka picked up the radio, signaling for ground control. No response came. Something was wrong with the transmitter.

Mishenka pulled back the panel to see if repairs could be made. There was nothing there. No circuitry. No components. Nothing. It was an empty device with a façade for a control panel. More cost saving efforts.

Never having feared death for being forever cursed never to experience it, Mishenka didn't waver. He knew there was but one option that remained. He flipped back the clear plastic protecting barrier to reveal the self-destruct button.

The real tragedy, he thought, was that the explosion wouldn't actually end his existence. Mishenka hit the red button. Boom.

*(Mishenka Belov hosts "31 Dystopian Realms for October".)*

What other calamities does the Undead Cosmonaut capitulate?

*Find out as he takes you through…*

# 31 Dystopian Realms FOR OCTOBER

**also from**

**Mandy Pullman Publishing**

# GIVING UP THE GHOST

Adélaïde Rieux finished her 31 spells for October and breathed her last. The effort had been too much for the old witch.

The werewolf broke free of the paralytic spell, bolting off into the cold November morning. It didn't give a second glance to the body of the witch for fear of trickery. It howled a song of freedom which trailed off into nothingness.

The body looked like it had been decomposing for weeks, though it had only been a couple hours since the soul departed. The glossy white eyes finally saw nothing at all. She was dead.

Across the country, and even through some parts of the world, the spells she had cast lost their tenuous grip with reality and split apart at the seams. For many, this was for the better. For a few, it was infinitely worse. The magic died with the witch.

But Adélaïde was finally free. She could even see her body on the floor as she ascended into the heavens. Or, more likely, took the express elevator down.

What she hadn't expected was for neither to occur. She waited around, trying to figure out where to go. When no options presented themselves, Adélaïde groaned.

After another moment, she realized she didn't want to sit around with a corpse – even if it was her own body. Best she do something about this afterlife jazz herself. Adélaïde left the shack, headed for the main road into town. Perhaps, she considered, she could hitchhike to Heaven.

The trek through the swamps to the highway was the easiest it had been in years. Perhaps there was something to this afterlife, after all. She smiled.

After walking down the dirt road for a while, she heard a rumble of a distant engine followed by the twin headlight beams. Adélaïde turned to the approaching vehicle, sticking out her thumb.

The car slowed and Adélaïde thought she had caught a break. A man with wide eyes shivered as he yelled, "A ghost!".

He hit the gas and the car careened down the road, barely staying on it.

"Figures," she muttered, "a ghost."

With that, she continued down the road trying to decide who to haunt first.

# ACKNOWLEDGEMENTS

*Cover Image*

Spellbook, courtesy of Pixabay.com.

*Stories*

"Aunt Doris and the Hall Closet" first appeared in Fright Feast IV, 2014.

"Board Stiffs" first appeared on the CreepyGram and the Mourning Show podcast, episode 19 - "Paranormal Distribution", March 6, 2018.

"Bogwater" first appeared in Fright Feast I, 2012.

"Breadcrumbs" first appeared on the CreepyGram and the Mourning Show podcast, episode 98 - "Frights of Fancy", December 6, 2018.

"Chalkman" first appeared on the CreepyGram and the Mourning Show podcast, episode 56 - "Creepypasta with Extra Cheese", July 2, 2018.

"Copper Ants" first appeared in Fright Feast II, 2013.

"Curse of Wingate Mansion" first appeared in Fright Feast III, 2013.

"Death Pact" first appeared in Fright Feast III, 2013.

"Drip Drip" first appeared in Fright Feast IV, 2014.

"Finish the Story, Grandpa" first appeared on the CreepyGram and the Mourning Show podcast, episode 31 - "Mythical Monstrosities", April 17, 2018.

"House Wine" first appeared in Fright Feast III, 2013.

"Lair of the Mandrake" first appeared on the CreepyGram and the Mourning Show podcast, episode 23 - "Monstrous Circumstances", March 20, 2018.

"Matryoshka" first appeared on the CreepyGram and the Mourning Show podcast, episode 80 - "Unlikely Allies", October 4, 2018.

"Robert Johnson's Barter" first appeared on the CreepyGram and the Mourning Show podcast, episode 8 - "Speak of the Devil", January 25, 2018.

"Shapeshifter" first appeared on the CreepyGram and the Mourning Show podcast, episode 49 - "It's Only Supernatural", June 19, 2018.

"Sins of the Father" first appeared on the CreepyGram and the Mourning Show podcast, episode 9 - "Family Matters", January 30, 2018.

"Smoke Dancer" first appeared in Campfire Legends: Vol. 2 (Trick-or-Treat Thrillers Book 15), October, 2022

"Something Familiar" first appeared on the CreepyGram and the Mourning Show podcast, episode 6 - "Dishonor Bound", January 18, 2018.

"Spoiled" first appeared on the CreepyGram and the Mourning Show podcast, episode 26 - "Witch Side is Your Bread Buttered On?", March 29, 2018.

"Still Life and Death" first appeared on the CreepyGram and the Mourning Show podcast, episode 12 - "Curses, Foiled Again!", February 8, 2018.

"The Clawfoot Bathtub" first appeared on the CreepyGram and the Mourning

Show podcast, episode 12 - "Curses, Foiled Again!", February 8, 2018.

"The Cursed Audiocassette" first appeared on the CreepyGram and the Mourning Show podcast, episode 25 - "Urban Legends", March 27, 2018.

"The Ghost Who Solved Her Own Murder" first appeared on the CreepyGram and the Mourning Show podcast, episode 101 - "Spectral Surprises", December 18, 2018.

"The Warlock's Garden" first appeared on the CreepyGram and the Mourning Show podcast, episode 26 - "Witch Side is Your Bread Buttered On?", March 29, 2018.

"There's Someone in the House" first appeared on the CreepyGram and the Mourning Show podcast, episode 80 - "Unlikely Allies", October 4, 2018.

"Things of Sand and Sweat" first appeared on the CreepyGram and the Mourning Show podcast, episode 59 - "Straight Road Trippin'", July 24, 2018.

"Unreal Estate" first appeared on the CreepyGram and the Mourning Show podcast, episode 94 - "Feasting on Fear", November 22, 2018.

"What Ales You" first appeared on the CreepyGram and the Mourning Show podcast, episode 92 - "The Unusual Suspects?", November 15, 2018.

"Where Did You Bury Me?" first appeared on the CreepyGram and the Mourning Show podcast, episode 17 - "Legend Has It", February 27, 2018.

"Yellow Car" first appeared on the CreepyGram and the Mourning Show podcast, episode 28 - "Just Desserts", April 5, 2018.